The Nameless

I: A Journey Begins

BELLAVISTA

I

A Journey Begins

ISBN: 9798844424793

Introduction

New York. The Big Apple. Life pulsated in this mega city. Here, the flow of people never seemed to stop. During the day, the streets and offices were busy with people who go to work, and the subway was full of these hard-working employees in the morning. When evening came, these people disappeared into their houses and locked their doors with security chains because fear was omnipresent. The night began. In dark backyards and alleys, other people came out of their homes. Almost everyone who was dirty moved in the shade of their houses. They were dealers, murderers, and prostitutes. In short, the scums!

Not a single night passed when the police didn't have to leave to bring these people to their senses. Other laws prevailed in the darkness. Those people, who did not pay attention, were pushed into the maelstrom of violence. Some found themselves shot in the gutter and, of course, nobody had seen it. That was New York, a paradise and hell on Earth.

Chapter 1

Month of May. It was eight o'clock in the morning. The male figure turned around the block and walked towards a house. This man had been out all-night cleaning up the street canyons of New York. His name was Erik Fenton. Detective Erik Fenton, to be more precise. He works in the Brooklyn Police District, which is half an hour's walk from his apartment. He lives near Slocum Place in the Kensington district near Brooklyn. Erik walked along the sidewalk and drove his right hand over his face.

For his age, he still looked very attractive. He was thirty-nine years old and had a hard, well-trained body. His skin color was white and had dark blonde short hair. His height was 1.80 meters, and he weighed 160 pounds (73 kilogram). 'There goes another night,' he thought and reached the entrance of the house. He stopped in front of the entrance and grabbed his hair.

"Oh no, please don't," he said. What he saw on the street, next to the house, was not to his liking at all. A construction site had been built there and the workers were already coming. He walked towards the front door and entered the house. He walked through the hallway to the stairs and reached the third floor. There, he opened the apartment door and entered. He closed it behind him. He took off his clothes and laid them over the sofa. Then he went into the bedroom, closed the curtains and closed the window. In the semi-dark room, he slipped under the blanket. He laid the pillow over his head. It was of no use.

On the street, the concrete was torn open with a pneumatic drill. Despite the closed windows, he heard the hammering and vibrating of the construction. His whole body vibrated along with it. "Damn!" he cursed under the pillow. "I can't even sleep here". All morning and afternoon, he heard the noise from the street. At some point he fell asleep, but it didn't take long because the alarm clock rang.

He muttered "This damn clock, too". He fumbled with his right hand for the alarm clock and made it shut up. Fenton stayed in bed for a few minutes until he picked himself up and shuffled into the bathroom. There, he took a hot shower and ate some bread after. Between, he had dressed for the night shift he had for this week. It wasn't a police uniform. No! He was dressed in civilian clothes and was wearing dark trousers, a shirt with a tie and a jacket. He also had a dark blue raincoat on when he left the house. It was already dark outside. He walked through the streets of Brooklyn and approached the Police Station. He preferred this place and liked to work here more than at the 70th police station. A year ago, there had been a bad incident with the local police. A 30-year-old black man had been beaten and tortured in a toilet. Four police officers were arrested and reported; the commander of the precinct and his deputy were dismissed and the police officer on duty was suspended.

At that time, the mayor of New York promised to crack down on the police. Today, after he was re-elected, everything remained the same. Not much had changed. Erik shook his head and didn't want to think about this case anymore. He approached the guard and heard screams. The closer he came, the louder they became. Two cops dragged a guy to the guard. He must have eaten something out, otherwise they wouldn't touch him so hard. He yelled at them and kicked them. Soon, the two cops had dragged the guy into the precinct and calmness returned to the street. Eric Fenton shook his head. 'There are days when you shouldn't get up from bed,' he thought. How right could he be because he didn't know what was coming to him that night.

Chapter 2

Somewhere in Queens. There was a black van in the garage. Two guys were sitting in the front seats of the car. One guy was wearing dark jeans, a checkered shirt and a leather jacket. He had short hair which was now covered by a knitted cap. The face looked like a rat. It was pointy and he wore a puny muzzle. His name was Max Conti. The other guy wore blue jeans, a dark blue sweater and a leather jacket. His face was roundish, as was his body. Like his partner, he wore a knitted wool cap on his head. His name was Phil Travis. Both held firearms in their hands and were checking them. The drum was full. In each chamber was the deadly lead bullets. Max Conti had them turned and folded them into the gun. , Phil Travis was ready and put them, like his partner, into his leather jacket. "Let's go!" hissed Conti. That was the sign for Travis. He, sitting at the wheel, turned the ignition key. The car started immediately with a full sound. The garage door had been opened earlier. The van left the garage and drove backwards onto the road. Then, Travis engaged the first gear and the truck started. The light from the spotlights broke through the darkness when he turned it on. They drove across the Bronx and reached Brooklyn. A police car overtook them once. This one took no notice of them because they were after a tempo finder.

"Once again, I was lucky," Travis said, holding the wheel tightly.

"Calm down," spoke Conti. "What we need now is a cool head".

"Okay, okay. I already have myself under control". Phil Travis still reeked of sweat under his clothes. The presence of the cops made him more nervous than he admitted. The ride ended after an hour and a half in Brooklyn. The van drove slowly through Foster Avenue. Travis held the truck in front of a lattice bridle. Behind it stood the Brooklyn Terminal Market. Only the area was reasonably illuminated. The whole surrounding area was lost in the darkness.

"Go, get out of the car!" hissed Conti, who played as the leader. "Everything has to go according to plan. Otherwise, we'll be delivered". They both left the van. They let the doors fall quietly into the castle and looked around to see if nobody had seen them.

"The air is clear. Come on! Cut through the fence". Travis held a pair of pincers in his hand that he had previously pulled out from under the driver's seat. He stuck it between the meshes and squeezed the two handles together. The grid could be cut like butter. One metal stitch after the other he cut apart, until the hole was big enough to slip through. Conti was keeping an eye on the surroundings.

"I am ready," Travis whispered and dropped the pliers. It fell to the ground next to the car, clattering a little.

"Idiot!" cursed Conti. "Do you want to have spectators?"

"Sorry. It was not my intention". Conti said nothing. He squeezed through the hole in the fence and stood on the other side.

"What is it!? Do you need an invitation?" Travis followed him and both stalked quietly towards the building. Everything was quiet. No one had heard anything before. In spite of the light that prevailed here on this site, both reached the building unseen. They walked along the wall one behind the other until they reached the corner of the house. Conti looked around them and his gaze caught the television camera. It was about three meters above the floor, firmly screwed into the wall. The light above the housing shone. It was on and the lens pointed down where the door was. There was the staff entrance and exit to the market.

"Curse it!" hissed Conti. He had looked away again. "The door isn't moving. The guy set us up".

Normally, the camera had to move back and forth. That wasn't the case here. "What do we do now?" Travis asked.

"Well, what do you think? We risk it! Okay?" Conti said. Travis stayed silent. If they wanted to succeed, they had to risk it. Conti took a deep breath and said: "You stay here. I go first. When I call, you come after me!" He turned around to the corner, ran off and reached the door after a few steps. Then a little further, and he stood under the camera.

'Hopefully, nobody saw me,' he thought and breathed out the air. He had a small tool bag tied around his stomach. He opened the zipper and pulled out a screwdriver. With this, he approached the fuse box on the wall under the camera at eye level. The screws were on the four corners. He unscrewed them and removed the metal cover. Quietly, he laid it on the floor in front of him. The wires in the fuse box were crosswise over and below each other. He took a pair of pliers out of the tool bag and looked for the red wire. He found it behind the other wires. With the pliers, he cut it and the light over the housing of the camera went out. He signaled, "All clear," quietly to his buddy. "You can come". Travis turned around the corner and joined Conti.

"Now, the door," hissed Conti. With a special burglary tool, he took out of his pocket, he unlocked the door lock within seconds. The entrance was open. He let his tool disappear into his pocket.

"Go in and don't make a sound". Travis was the first to cross the threshold. Conti followed him and closed the door behind him. Both of them took a flashlight from the leather jackets. They turned it on at the same time and the beam hit the ground. Now they slowly moved forward and walked along the long corridor in front of them. The light of the torches kept breaking through the darkness. Conti pointed the beam to the right. There was a door through which one could enter the Market. Travis was already there and opened it . He looked through the narrow gap and saw only darkness. No one was there. He opened the door completely and both crooks slipped into the market. They knew their way around here pretty well, because they had been here before. They crept quietly through the hall. Down here was the vegetable and fruit section. It smelled very appetizing. Travis came by a stand offering fresh apples. He grabbed one and bit it with great pleasure.

"You must be crazy, you idiot!" hissed Conti. "You can't have a picnic here. We came here because of something else!"

"Shut up!" Travis resisted. "You never let me have any fun and don't call me an idiot. You idiot!"

"I will show you who's the idiot". Conti hit him with the flashlight on the head.

"Ow! Are you crazy?" whispered Travis, who dropped the apple and drove his left hand over his head. He felt little pain under the wool cap.

"Go on and don't do anymore nonsense". Conti pushed his partner forward. There were the escalators leading to the upper floors. They walked up quietly and listened to every sound. Moments later, they reached the upper floor. They stepped to the left, then to the right and immediately stood in front of a door.

"That's it," whispered Conti. "Behind it, there is a lot of money". He took his tools out of his pocket and wanted to crack the door lock after putting his flashlight away. Travis held his flashlight in his hand. The beam hit the door lock. Conti could work in peace.

Chapter 3

At the mall's security room, Mike Flint was sitting in a comfortable armchair. On this chair, he had spent the last ten years. He was the supermarket guard. Not one day had he stayed away. Like a Swiss watch, he arrived on time every evening and replaced his colleague on the day shift. He was over sixty years old. His hair was already white and his face wrinkled for years. The uniform matched his slender body. As I said, he sat in his armchair and monitored the monitors of the outdoor cameras. At some point, he'd had enough of looking and turned around. He grabbed a magazine lying behind him on a shelf and leafed through it. He was looking at a report on the first baseball game of the season.

"Hey, Man," he spoke to himself. "These fools can't even win the first game".

He was a New York Yankee fan through and through. He turned to the monitors and immediately put the magazine in front of him on the table. What he saw next was suspicious. A security monitor had failed. It showed no picture from the outside camera. He turned the buttons of the box. Nothing! The picture remained pitch black. 'Something's wrong,' he thought and got up. He grabbed the flashlight next to him on the table and walked out of the small room. He left the door open. Subsequently, a little fresh air could enter the room. Flint was in an attached building complex of the Market. Through a staircase that led down he reached the outside. There, he walked around the block and saw the staff entrance and exit. What immediately caught his eye as he approached was that the metal cover of the fuse box was on the floor. He also examined the wires in the box and discovered that one had been cut. This was the connection for the outdoor camera. Now he realized that someone had sabotaged this connection. His gaze wandered to the right; the door. He approached it and turned the door knob to the left. It was not locked. He opened it and penetrated into the darkness. He quietly closed it behind him again and turned on the flashlight he was holding in his left hand. With his right hand, he grabbed the weapon holder hanging from his belt. He pulled out his gun and unlocked it. Then, he walked through the corridor and soon reached the vegetable and fruit section. With the light of the lamp, he illuminated all the corners until the beam hit the ground. The suspicion that someone was there hardened. There was a bitten apple on the floor. 'Look at that. It appears someone is here after all,' he thought. 'I also think I know where that someone is now'. He walked slowly towards the escalator and reached the upper floor through it. He had switched off the light from his flashlight before. The security could also make good progress in the dark because he knew this building very well. Even from a distance, he could hear someone talking quietly. 'It must have been several people who broke in here,' were his thoughts. On tiptoes, he approached the voices and discovered two men about to break into the payroll office door. One held a flashlight in his hand and shone on the doorknob. The other one was tampering with the lock. Mike Flint wanted to spoil this break-in for them. He approached them without Being heard. Then, he took action.

Chapter 4

Hold the light still. You wiggle around with it as if you had tremor attacks," complained Conti who did not hit the lock with the tool. "Oh, fuck me!" said Travis, who'd had enough of being plunged by Conti. He kept the light on the doorknob, but that changed in a few moments. They heard a voice from the darkness speaking to them. Accordingly, both flinched at the same time.

"Did I catch you?" Mike Flint said. He turned on the flashlight and the beam caught the two burglars.

"No sudden movement. Get away from the door! Quickly! Or do you need an invitation?" He held his gun in his right hand. It pointed in the direction of the Crooks. Conti blinked at Travis. He knew what to do. He waited for the next sign from him and the sign came. Conti dropped his tool. It clattered on the ground. Then, he reached into the left inside pocket of his leather jacket and pulled out his gun. The guard couldn't see it because he turned half his back towards him. He held it ready in his hand and nodded to his partner. "Didn't you hear what I said? Go! Go already or am I not clear enough?!"

"Okay. Okay. We'll do it," Travis said. He turned around and blinded the guard with the light of his flashlight. At that moment, Mike Flint was completely surprised by this action. He saw nothing more.

"What is this nonsense?" he said.

"No nonsense," said Conti, who pulled out his gun and aimed at the man. Mike Flint knew he had to do something. He fired from his service weapon and only hit the door, irritated by the flashlight light he saw nothing. The bullet got stuck in the wood. His firing was returned. Conti had pulled the trigger and hit the man right in the heart. The bullet came out on the guard's back, with a blood surge, and got lost in the dark. Mike

Flint's chest burned like fire. He couldn't hold the flashlight and it fell to the ground. He grabbed the chest with his left hand. Right where he felt the pain. He rattled and his service weapon also fell to the ground. Then, he tilted forward and hit the ground. He noticed his body weakening and weakening. His eyes closed and he fell into a dark tunnel from which there was no return. Mike Flint was dead. It took a few moments for the two men to wake up from their stiffness.

"Damn!" cursed Travis. "Why did this have to happen?" and looked at Conti reproachfully.

"Close your mouth. Just shut your mouth. Go! We have to get out of here quickly. Someone must have heard the shot". He bent down, picked up his tool and let it disappear into his tool bag. Subsequently, the two of them set off right away. They chased down the escalators and left the market after a few minutes. They ran through the grounds to the fence as if the devil was after them. They slipped through the hole in the fence and got into the van. Travis pushed the car key into the lock and turned it. The engine started and they drove off. Travis dripped sweat excessively. It wasn't just the sweat due to the race. No, he also sweated because he was afraid of getting caught. That could cost him another few years in prison, since he had already been inside once. There, he had also met Conti.

"Damn!" he cursed again and hit the steering wheel with his right hand. "I thought that you only wanted to hurt him. But that...!"

"You thought wrong," said Conti. "There is only one law. Him or us. Which variant do you like best?" He looked at his partner from the side. Travis said nothing. He drove and thought about many things. The streets were empty. No car drove after them and none met them. That was a good thing. That's why they preferred the side streets, where nothing was going on.

"Coward. Sissy," spoke Conti and shook his head. He shouldn't have said that. That was the trigger for Travis.

"You fucking asshole!" he screamed and clenched his right fist to the right. He caught Conti right in the face. This one howled open. He reached into the inside pocket of his leather jacket and pulled out his gun. He aimed to the left at his partner.

"You'll pay me for that," and closed his bleeding nose with his fingers. Travis saw what he was up to and looked at him angrily. He didn't even notice that he lost the road out of his eye. He also didn't notice that his foot was pushing the accelerator pedal lower. The car got faster. He concentrated on his partner and all he heard was him screaming.

"Watch out!" he screamed as he looked forward for a moment.

Travis looked at the poorly lit road and saw a figure standing in the middle of the road. With his mind alert, he tore the wheel hard to the right. The car began to skid. The figure tore his arms up as he saw the spotlights dazzle before his eyes. It was also a gesture, as if he wanted to fend off the car and protect himself from it. But against this monster on wheels, no flesh and blood creature could compete. The wagon hurled towards the figure. While turning, it hit the figure full of the tail. First, he was thrown up and then thrown away. Somewhere on the left side of the road the figure crashed to the ground and remained motionless. The car continued to slide despite Travis's counter-steering. He already had one turn behind him and the second came. The car approached the side of the road and shot over it. The two men heard screams. Until they noticed that they had been the ones screaming. Their screams mixed with the noise of a shattering window. The wagon had driven into a light mast. The windshield burst into a thousand pieces. Metal bent into each other, gropingly grating. The two were thrown forward. Conti fell through the windshield from the van. He hit the ground hard. Travis remained in the driver's seat. His head was hit on the steering wheel. Several minutes passed when one of the two stirred. It was Travis. He groaned loudly as he grabbed his head with his right hand. He felt a sticky liquid run over his fingers. "Oh, damn it! That hurts!" He looked at his hand and saw the blood.

"Shit!" was his next word and wiped the blood off his leather jacket. He looked to the right and didn't see his partner anymore. He discovered only fragments of the windshield scattered over the seat. He saw Conti's weapon lying on the ground. He had dropped it during the impact. But where was Conti? He bent forward and discovered him on the sidewalk. With his back, he lay on the ground and moved now. He supported himself with his hands and straightened his upper body. Slowly he turned to the side and stood up in slow motion. As he stood, he moved his head to shake off the dizzy spell he had now. With his left hand, he supported himself on the light pole. In some places, his body hurt. Still with staggering movements, he slowly stepped towards the wagon. Under his shoes, countless glass splinters of the windshield crunched. He saw Phil Travis sitting behind the wheel. He waved to him.

He spoke "Come," quietly. "Get in". Conti stepped towards the door and wanted to open it. He didn't get there. He heard a ripple.

'That's not normal,' he thought and looked down. He saw that water was flowing onto the sidewalk under the wagon. Water smelled of nothing. This one did. That was petrol. He straightened up and wanted to warn his partner. "No! Stop!" Travis already turned the ignition key to start the car. From the lock, sparks sprayed, which flew everywhere. The sparks ignited the petrol. First it flickered, then the lower part of the car burned. Conti screamed "Get out of there!" and ran away as fast as he could. Travis was still sitting behind the wheel. He noticed the smoke, then the fire that struck in front of him. He couldn't get through the door because it was too bent. Subsequently, he had to climb through the window. The heat was a problem for him. The flames that were beating higher scared him. He dared anyway, because he didn't want to be grilled. Like the wind, he climbed out of the car and ran behind his partner. Not a second too late, because the car went up in flames. It exploded and a huge jet of flame shot into the sky. This was covered by the black smoke that had formed. The car was still burning as they watched it from a safe distance. They also heard the sirens of the police approaching.

"Come on! We're getting out of here!" said Conti. They turned around and ran away as fast as they could. They simply left the figure they had hit lying there. The two did not know that something was set in motion through their fault. Perhaps this could mean the downfall of humanity.

Chapter 5

Erik Fenton was driving the company car in Brooklyn. A colleague was with him. His real partner was at home with spring flu. The night had started hours ago. It was around one o'clock in the morning when the radio signal came into the car: "Car 29. Please report".

Detective Fenton picked up the radio and pressed the trigger on the microphone. "Hello, headquarters. Here, car 29! What's up?"

"An emergency call came in. Explosion near Truxton Park. You are on this route so see what's going on."

"We understood! We're on our way. End!" There was an extra separate small pocket on the console. He put the mic back into it.

"You heard it. Then go," he said to the driver.

"I'm already on the way," said the latter. At the console was an extra separate small bag. He put the microphone back into it.

"You heard the man. Let's go," he said to the driver.

"I am already on the way," he said. He turned the wheel to the left and drove back the distance driven. Meanwhile, Erik Fenton stuck the red light on the roof of the car. This was held in place with a magnet. The siren was also switched on. The driver turned right into the road and both saw the sky full of black smoke from a distance, despite the darkness.

"There must be something going on," said the driver. He stopped the car behind the burning van. Both jumped out and approached it. Erik Fenton was the first to discover the motionless body of a figure. He was to his left. He ran towards him and looked at him. It was a male bum and he smelled the part. But he was a person who needed immediate help and he called over to his colleague. "Quickly! Call an ambulance!"

The colleague ran back to the car and called. Then, he walked to the rear of his company car and opened the trunk. There, he removed the fire extinguisher and ran back to the burning van. He tried to contain the fire with the white foam, which he failed to do. The fire brigade, which had arrived, now extinguished the fire. A small fire brigade entered the area and immediately set to work. The ambulance also arrived. Fenton called, "Here!" and waved with his hand kneeling next to the man. The bum wore a warm padded coat. There was a hat on the floor and an old brown leather backpack. The face was hidden behind a white beard. His head hair was also white. He kept his eyes closed. The paramedics rushed over and looked at the bum. They had taken the mobile stretcher with them.

"Looks bad. He is breathing very weakly," said one of the paramedics.

"Then let's go! Let's turn him on his back and then lay him on the stretcher," the other one said. As the ambulance drove away, Detective Fenton was still standing where he had found the man. He was worried about this man. 'Why was he lying here? Why was he hurt? Is he responsible for the burning car?' Questions to which he had no answer. He stepped back to the company car and stopped there. His colleague also stood there and watched the men of the fire brigade. The car was no longer burning. They had extinguished it.

"I think that forensics should have a look at the burnt-out wreck" Fenton said.

"Already in progress. I requested it earlier".

"That's good," Fenton said and rubbed the fingertips of his right hand.

"What have you got?" asked the colleague. "You have rubbed your fingers against each other as if they were sticky for a long time".

"They are not. It's just that...?"

"What then?"

"I don't know. It's weird. When I touched the bum, I got an electric shock. I only get it when I have cleaned the carpet in my apartment with a vacuüm cleaner or through the friction of clothes".

"I know that too," said the man next to him.

"But here...? There's no carpet here nor any source of friction and yet it was a small electrostatic charge emanating from this man".

"Maybe it was also your clothes. You rubbed your hands on it and then...?"

"I don't think so," said Erik Fenton. After about a quarter of an hour, the forensic team arrived. They moved towards the van. A fireman standing there approached them. He said, "I think this belongs to you," and rolled the water hose back together. "Looks like the gas has ignited."

"Thank you for the information," spoke one of the men and set to work like the other three. The van was coal-black and wet. Water dripped down from the roof. One of the men who ventured inside got a few drops in his neck. They ran down into his back. He felt it so wet and unpleasant that it made him shiver.

He said, "Brr!" and found what he was looking for. He took special gloves out of his jacket and reached for the floor of the car. There he grabbed a gun lying there. He lifted it up and shouted, "I found something!" Then he ran to the others. "Well, who do we have here? A Smith & Wesson. 9 millimeters," said one of the men.

"Put it in the plastic container. We'll look at it in the lab when we're done here". The man walked to his car. He opened the trunk and put the gun in a small container. Then he closed it and joined the others who had put forward a theory. Detective Fenton was there.
"From the looks of it, the car skidded. I looked at the tire tracks. The injured man must have tried to cross the road. He must have been caught by the tail of the van. This can be clearly seen at the rear of the burnt-out car. There's a bump in the metal that couldn't possibly have been caused by the impact. The driver or drivers are missing every trace," spoke one of the men of the forensic department.

"He or she ran away and simply left the old man lying there. If I can get my hands on him, he should ask mercy from God" Fenton said, gritting his teeth. For him, it was a promise.

"Very well. Let's get out of here," one of the men said. "Our work is finished here."

The four men got into the car. "Listen up!" Fenton bent down to the window. "Call me at this number. I want to know who owns the gun you found. Can you do that?" He gave one of the men his business card and they immediately drove away. Then he stepped back to the company car. The other colleague had already got in. Fenton also followed.

"Let's drive around the block a bit. Maybe we'll find who caused the accident".

"Okay," said the driver drove off. In the rear-view mirror, he saw the towing service arrive. This would take the van away. Soon the road would look the same as before. Except for the glass splinters on the floor and the broken light pole, it indicated that an accident had happened there.

Chapter 6

Hours later. It was about half past Four in the morning. Detective Erik Fenton was out on the streets of New York with his colleague. He stopped the car many times and asked the local people if they had seen anyone who had run away from the scene of the accident. Or who the social case (bum) was who was hit by the car. No one could tell him anything until he came across a guy who could give him some information. The man was spindly and small. His hair fell greasy and long on his shoulders. He had hardly any teeth when he opened his mouth.

"I heard from a guy that someone saw something," he spoke with a rough voice. In between, he coughed and lit a cigarette.

He spoke "Ahh!" with relish. "The first train is the best," and the smoke blew out.

"Who is the one who saw what?" asked Fenton.

"I don't know the name, but he wears a dark red scarf and is currently in the pennants' home, two blocks away".

"It's a homeless guy?"

"Of course. The bums all know each other and if one of them gets caught, then everyone knows".

"Okay. Thanks for the information," said Fenton and wanted to leave.

"Hey!" called the drought. "Not so fast. That'll cost you ten bucks for the info," and rubbed his right fingertips against each other. Detective Fenton grabbed his right hand in his trouser pocket and pulled out a ten-dollar bill.

"Here!" he stretched out the bill towards him. "The next info is free. Okay?

"Yes, yes. All right," the guy grumbled and made the bill disappear. Erik Fenton left and soon got into the car, which was a few meters further ahead.

"And did you succeed?" asked the colleague.

"Yes. We have to go two blocks to the homeless shelter."

"I know that place,"" said the driver and started the engine. After a good fifteen minutes, they arrived there. They got out of the car and entered the house. Here it smelled of everything. The worst were the human stench and the smell of alcohol, which was heavy in the air.

"The devil stinks. Here you can catch alcohol poisoning without having to drunk a sip".

"Indeed," Fenton said, holding his hand in front of his mouth. Eventually, he could inhale better. Through a narrow corridor, they came to a door. Behind this door, it went to the right and the two entered a large dining room. They stopped and looked into the room. Despite the early morning hours, Fenton was surprised to see so many stranded existences. Some of the homeless were sitting at the table slurping a broth that looked like soup. Others had put their heads on the tabletop and slept out their intoxication. Some were talking.

'What a sad sight. Poor people,' thought Erik Fenton as he saw these people.

"Can I help you?" asked a female voice. The voice ripped him from his thoughts. He turned his head to the left and looked into the eyes of a robust woman.

"Yes, I am Detective Fenton. This is a colleague of mine. I'm looking for someone wearing a dark red scarf".

"I am the director of the home. Pleased to meet you," the woman said. "My name is Samantha Peel, but everyone calls me Sam. It's easier".

She shook hands with the detective. "You're looking for someone with a dark red scarf?"

"I've already said that".

"Then only Smithy comes into question. He's sitting back there in the corner, but he's not doing so well today. He is so silent. That's unusual".

"Thank you," said Fenton and took a step forward.

"Has he eaten something out?" Sam asked.

"I don't know? Let's see". The two men walked around the tables and stopped in front of the man who called himself Smithy.

"Hello, Smithy," spoke to him Erik Fenton. "How are you?" The homeless man held a cup of black coffee in it with both dirty hands to warm himself. He was wearing a thick coat over a jacket. The face was hidden behind a beard. Eyes straightened, as if looking into the distance.

"He is totally absent-minded," said the colleague.

"What am I again, you fucker? Who are you anyway? What do you want?" Smithy blurted out. Erik Fenton showed him his ID. "Cops? That, I'm not laughing. Where were you when I needed you the most?" he murmured the last sentence and took a sip from the cup.

"When did you need it?" asked Fenton.

"Oh, someday".
"I don't think so. You would have needed us a few hours ago when the accident happened. Didn't you?" He kept quiet. But then, he spoke up.

"Yes, damn it. My friend got it and I don't know if he is still alive".

"I don't know either, but I'll let you know. Now you tell us what you saw".

He thought for a moment before continuing. "I stood about thirty meters away. That's at the street corner. My friend ran across the street when the van came up to him. The truck hurled and caught my friend. He didn't even scream when he was hit".

"Who was driving the car?" asked Fenton.

"Two guys ran away shortly after. But they must have gotten something when they hit the mast pole. I can't say any more". He took another sip from the cup.

"Why didn't you stay there? You could have contacted us later when we were there".

"I was afraid. Not from you, but from the burning wagon and the two of them. Who knows what they would have done to me. A bum's life is worth nothing today".

"I understand," said Fenton.

"Okay. Thank you for the information," the colleague said.

Smithy nodded. When the two cops wanted to leave, he spoke to them again.

"Don't forget to let me know if my friend gets better."

Erik Fenton turned around and asked, "What's your friend's name?"

"Nobody knows his first name. We call him Gun-he abbreviation of his surname Gunnarsson". Something clicked in Fenton's head.

'I've heard that name before. But where...?' he thought and shook his head as if he wanted it out of this one.

"What is it?" asked the colleague

"Nothing. Let's go." Both left the homeless shelter and drove back to the Brooklyn Police District. Maybe they had already found out something from forensics. A quarter of an hour later, Fenton knew. The file he read was extensive. The fingerprints on the gun belonged to a guy named Max Conti.

"Look at that," Fenton murmured. "It was that rat Conti who caused the accident". He reached for the phone and had an arrest warrant issued. The address was fed into the house computer, but Conti could disappear everywhere. Subsequently, it was pointless to go there now to see if he was really there. He issued a manhunt. Maybe the colleagues, who had shift on the day, had more luck and could find out where Conti was at the moment. It was morning again and Erik Fenton made his way home. Maybe today he could sleep through the day without being woken up by the noise of the street.

Chapter 7

It was about ten o'clock in the morning when Erik Fenton's eyelids began to vibrate. He moved his head from left to right. The room was warm and small drops of sweat had formed on his forehead. He was dreaming. It was more like a memory from his childhood. He saw himself again as a little boy of four years. With his short legs, he ran across a lawn towards someone. This someone stood in front of a garden fence and turned his back towards him. It was a woman he was running towards. "Ma'am!" he shouted.

She turned around, kneeled down briefly, opened her arms and lifted the little man up. Then she turned around again and looked forward. Her gaze was on a man who was twenty meters away from her. The woman held the child on her right arm. She raised her left arm. She waved goodbye to the man who was leaving. Now she turned her arm again and her hand approached her face. From her eyes, tears rolled down. With her hand, she wiped them away. The hand was still there when she pressed it onto her mouth and whispered a little. Despite the whisper, the little boy heard what it was. A name fell. A name he had heard only once and never again.

"Gunnarsson". Like a stab in the heart, Erik Fenton awoke from this dream. His heart pounded and the pulse raced wildly. The bed sheet was stuck to his naked upper body. A spot of sweat appeared on the sheet. Only now did the memory came back. This man must have had something to do with him. But what?

The only possibility was to question him. But before that, he had to do something else. His Mother had pronounced the name when he was little. Was there a connection between the two? He wanted to get to the bottom of this and jumped out of bed. After half an hour, he was on his way towards Oceanside. The destination was the retirement home where his Mother lived.

Chapter 8

It was a long drive that he had to overcome. First through the midday traffic, then past John F. Kennedy Airport and finally through the small outlying quarters, until he arrived in Oceanside in the late afternoon. He stopped the car in front of the old people's residence. It was a VW Golf with air conditioning. When he got out and approached the wooden house, he noticed the warmth. 'The air conditioning was good, but now the heat is beating me,' he thought and opened the top button of his shirt. He also loosened the tie. When he entered the main entrance of the old people's residence, he did not notice that his tie was hanging crooked.

"Oh, Mr. Fenton," spoke to him of a woman who met him.

He spoke to her, "Hello, Mrs. Taylor". She was the good soul of this house. "I'm looking for my Mother. Is she in her room?"

"No," said Mrs. Taylor. "On such a beautiful day, she can only be found in the garden".
"Thank you," Erik Fenton spoke and walked past the woman. He knew the way to the garden behind the house. Through a bright corridor he reached the back door and opened it. The view was overwhelming every time. 'Yes. You can really feel comfortable here,' he thought. It was a large meadow that opened before him. Some trees were also present. These provided shade and a pleasant coolness. Under the trees, some elderly people gathered to chat with each other. But the view was not over here. Further ahead was the Silver Lake Park and also the small lake. This idyll was something special for these people. It was a small paradise. After a few steps, Erik Fenton stood on the meadow. He had discovered his Mother further ahead. The grass dampened his steps as he approached her. She sat in a white chair by the small lake and looked over the water. Then she lowered her head and continued reading a book she held in her hands. When she heard a voice in her back, she stopped

reading.

"Hello, Mother," she only heard. She turned around and looked into her son's eyes.

"Erik," she only whispered. Then she stood up and put the book on the chair. First, she embraced him and then she kissed her son on the cheek. Almost every Sunday, Erik Fenton would drove here to visit her.

"What a surprise! But it's not Sunday. How do I get this honor?" she said. He just looked at her. For her sixty-five years, she was still very sprightly, dynamic and her mind still awake. Maybe that was because she read a lot and went for walks just as much. She wore her white hair open. She wore a light blouse and a dark brown skirt. The open shoes were the same color as the blouse.

"Come," said Erik "Sit down". She sat down on the chair again. Her son sat down on one of the big stones on the shore of the lake. The two looked at each other.

"I see in your eyes that something is bothering you," his Mother said.

"Hmm," Erik smiled. "You know me exactly, Mother. Nothing escapes you. Don't you?"

"You are my son. One cannot withhold anything from a Mother".

"How right you are".

"You have come here. It is surely not only a visit. So? Tell me what is going on. Does it have something to do with your work?"

"I believe it's both".

"What do you mean?"

"Like I said. With me and my work". Erik's Mother's gaze darkened.

"I don't understand," although she suspected something. She asked him to "Tell me".

"All right," he said. "Who was my father, really? I won't accept lies anymore, mother."

He had heard of her when he was still little that he had died in an accident. Erik looked into her eyes and saw how they looked to the ground. She sighed. He spoke to her "Mother," because she didn't say anything. Then he spoke to her again and dropped a name. For his Mother, this name was like a surge of electricity shooting through her body. "Gunnarsson". That was the trigger he was waiting for. The Mother, who had lowered her head, lifted it up and looked at her son. She cried. He took a fresh handkerchief out of his jacket and handed it to her. She wiped the tears from her eyes. They had turned red at the edges as she remembered the times gone by. Erik Fenton gave her time to recover. After a while, he spoke to her again. "Was my father's surname Gunnarsson?"

She just nodded and spoke to him. "How did you know his name? Who told you?"

"I'll tell you later. Tell me now what really happened back then".

She took a deep breath before she started talking. "I am so sorry that I had to lie to you all these years. Your father didn't die in an accident when you were little. He went away. He left us".

"Why only now?"

"Because I—No, we wanted it to be that way!"

"Mother," he spoke to her. Slowly but surely, she began to get on her nerves. He noticed that she didn't want to give up what she knew.

"I was young," she started. "Eighteen and a half years young. At that time, I lived with my parents in the country. That was in Cooperstown. A small town near the Catskill Mountains. I stood at the garden fence and looked towards the mountains. How much I enjoyed the view of these mountains, which I still miss today. From the corner of my eye I noticed a movement. I turned my head to the right and saw the figure approaching me. It was a young hiker who walked down the road and stepped on me after a few minutes. He asked me about the way to Wilkes Barre. Our eyes met and it was love at first sight. Yes! I had fallen in love with your father at that moment. He was tall, strong and three years older than me. You inherited the same hair color as him and he came from Northern Europe. Subsequently, as I said, we had fallen in love. But here on the farm he could not stay. My parents would have a fit of raving madness if a stranger was here in the house. That's why he stayed in a motel outside the village. During the day, we met at any time. These were wonderful hours we spent together. I was the happiest woman in the world. But then something came to us that we never dreamed of. I got pregnant. You were the child who saw the world nine months later."

"But why did I keep your maiden name and not my father's last name?" asked Erik Fenton.

"I wanted it that way. My husband, although we never got married, stayed with me until your third birthday. A few days later, he took me aside and talked about himself and the future. I noticed that something was wrong with him. Then he revealed his secret to me. From that day on, I understood what a burden he was carrying on his shoulders. On your fourth birthday, I stood at the garden fence. You were there too. I held you in my arms and we watched him for a long time as he slowly disappeared from our field of vision".

"What had been wrong with him?"

"That, I cannot tell you," she pressed quietly out. "I only know one thing. He left us. He left you and me alone. I will never forget what he did". Erik Fenton's innermost was stirred up. Did he hate his father or was it something else he thought about?

"Yes, he had left us, but he has never forgotten about us. He kept sending us money so that we could be well. He allowed you to do what I could not do. With the money, you could go to school and attend high school later. Then, you entered the police academy and were able to continue your education. Only with his help that you could achieve everything you are now. Thus, don't judge your father badly. He is a good person".

"I understand," said Erik thoughtfully.

"But what about you? You were alone and had me. It's not an easy task to raise me up".

"It was very difficult to be a single mother in these times. But you see, it went alright, nevertheless. Of course, your father wrote me as often as he could. In all the past years, I have received countless letters from him. They are in my room. I got the last letter half a year ago. I haven't heard or read from him since".

"I think I know where he is at the moment," said Erik.

"You know where he is? Tell me. Where is he?" said Erik's Mother excitedly.

"But I am not completely sure if it is him". Detective Fenton reached into his inner jacket pocket and pulled out a cell phone. He set the Police District number and called the colleague who was with him last night. "Hello, James. It's me Erik".

"Hi, Erik. Where are you?"

"In the Oceanside. But I'm calling for something completely different. Can you find out which hospital the injured man from last night was brought into?"

"Of course. Give me a minute. I'll call you back."

Erik Fenton gave him his mobile number and disconnected the call. Erik's Mother grabbed his chest. "My God!" pressed her out. "Is he hurt?". 'Damn!' thought Erik. He had said something about an injured person and did not think about his Mother at that moment. He had excited her unnecessarily. "A man was admitted to the hospital, but I don't know if he is father". The portable phone beeped. Erik answered. He said "Yes," briefly into the narrow thing.

"The man named Gunnarsson was admitted to the Brooklyn Hospital Center".

"Thank you, James," Fenton spoke and said goodbye again. He let the mobile phone disappear again into the inside pocket of his jacket. "It is getting late. I will go now, Mother".

"Where are you going?" she asked.

"To the hospital. I want to see who the man is. Maybe he is my father".

"No," she said, "I will go. I'll order a taxi and go there. You must not go. Promise me. Please". It was a plea from his Mother, but he didn't give up.

"Mother! What are you hiding from me?"

"You will not understand. I do not want you to come near him".

"Does it have anything to do with his secret?" She remained silent. That was the reaction he had been waiting for. Subsequently, he thought, 'Well, of course. It has something to do with his secret,' and this made him curious. "I will go now more than ever and you can't stop me, Mother". He got up. His Mother was still sitting on the chair.

"I beg you. Don't go there. Please!"

"Mother. My decision has been made. You can either come with me or you can stay here."

She stood up and grabbed her son by the arm. "I'll come with you. May God have mercy on us". Then she didn't speak a word anymore. The two of them walked through the meadow and entered the house. Minutes later, they were on their way.

Chapter 9

It was about eight o'clock in the evening when they arrived at the hospital. They went inside the house and asked the reception for the patient's room number. "No one is allowed to go there. He is in intensive care. Only family members are allowed there," the receptionist said. Erik Fenton showed his identity card. "It is possible that this man is my long-lost father. I beg you. Let us in. We would like to make sure that it is him". The woman at the reception sucked in air.

"All right. But no longer than ten minutes per person".

"Thank you," the Mother said. The woman at the reception, who was behind the wooden corpus, called for a night nurse to lead them to the room where the man was.

The nurse asked, "Are you his relatives?"

"We'll see about that," Fenton said. After the three had gone through the endless long corridors, they came to the intensive care unit. One room was next to the ward and some chairs were in front of the room.

"I want to be the first to go in," said Erik's Mother.

"Okay. I'll wait out here," he said. The older woman pushed the door trap down and entered the room. Then, she closed the door behind her. She was in the room with the injured man.

Chapter 10

Can you tell me who this patient's chief resident is?" asked Detective Fenton.

"Yes. That's Dr. Kerren," the nurse answered the question.

"Is he here?"

"Yes. He's supposed to be in one of the rooms we passed. Would you like to see him?"

"That would have been my next question."

"Just a moment. I'll see where he is right now," said the nurse. She was about to leave when she saw a man in a white coat coming out of a room. He turned his back to them.

"Dr. Kerren!" she shouted. The doctor turned around. "Can you please come here for a moment?" the woman said. The doctor nodded and started to move. After a few steps, he was with the both of them. The nurse introduced him to the detective and immediately left the two.

"Can you tell me how the patient inside is?"

"Unfortunately, he is in a very bad condition," said the doctor. "He might not make it with those injuries. He has internal bleeding. In addition, several ribs were broken. Two of them have pierced the lungs. He is, thus, artificially ventilated for now. His condition has stabilized, but this can change anytime. That's all we can do for the man. I'm so sorry". The doctor had told him the facts soberly and straight to his face.

Fenton paused for a moment and said, "I understand". Erik Fenton spoke quietly and sadly to himself.

For the man in the white coat, this short conversation was over. "If you'll excuse me," he said, "I still have to look for the other patients". He shook hands with the detective and walked away.

Erik whispered, "Yes, of course". He sat down on one of the chairs and waited for his Mother who was in the room with the man. Was the injured man really his father? He would certainly know when she comes out.

Chapter 11

Erik's Mother walked through the dimly lit room. Equipment was everywhere. Countless hoses and wires hung out of these apparatuses. The EEG (Electroencephalogram), which was also present, beeped quietly over the man. The man was lying on his back. There was a transparent tube on his face. This led to his nostrils and disappeared into them. One of the machines gave the man the oxygen he needed to inhale through his nose. The woman could see that much as she went to his bed. Now she stood at the end of the bed and looked at the older man. She raised her right hand to her mouth so as not to sob out loud. It was Erik Gunnarsson. The man she had always and still loved. Despite the white beard and the white hair, she could recognize him. His eyes were closed. His mouth was open, and he also sucked the air in. Somehow, he noticed that someone was in the room. His eyelids moved and slowly, he opened them. Despite the faint light, he recognized the figure at the end of the bed. It was a woman. He didn't know how long she had been standing there looking at him, but he recognized her. Quietly, he pronounced the name of the woman, "Eva…".

She nodded, "Yes," and went to the left side of the bed. "Yes, dear. It is me". The tears ran down her wall. At the side of the bed stood a chair. She sat down on it. She had her eyes turned towards the man's face. She raised her hands up and looked for the man's right hand. She clung tightly to his hand, which lay on the bed. It was as if her hands would never let go.

"Why are you crying?" he asked, quietly.

"I don't know. Because I finally found you? Or maybe because I am seeing you lying like that?" The man didn't say a word. He felt the woman's two warm hands. It was as if time, even the years, had never passed. He just looked deeply into her eyes. It was true love that she felt for him. It was also certain for him. His love for her had never extinguished. There were intimate moments which the two of them spent together without talking. Everyone followed their thoughts. Then, he interrupted the silence.

"How did you find me?" he wanted to know.

"It was Erik. Our son found you injured on the street". He had told her that on the way here.

"Erik?" he spoke excitedly. "Where is he?"

"He's in front of the door."

"Send him away. Please. He must not see me. He must not come near me". The man got upset. The EEG device started beeping. It reacted and struck at any unusual physical activity. The wave patterns in the monitor went up and down.

"Calm down," the woman said to the man. She kept holding his hand. After speaking several times, she succeeded in calming her husband. "I... I will try to convince Erik that you don't want to see him".

"That's good. Do everything in your power not to let him in".

"I'll try, darling". Then she got up, let go of his hand and bent towards him. Her lips touched his forehead and then his lips. It was a kiss of love. How often had she waited to feel his lips again? Then, she straightened up and surrounded the end of the bed. As she stood by the door, she turned around and spoke to him. "No matter what happens. I want you to know that I loved you and I still do, forever and always. Please get well again". She opened the door and left the room.

Chapter 12

Erik drove his hands over his hair. He sat bent forward on the chair and raised his upper body when he heard a click. It was his Mother who came out of the room and closed the door behind her. He stood up and looked at her. "Is he my father?" He could have saved himself that question. He saw the crying eyes of his Mother. 'Yes, it is him. I knew it,' he thought. The Mother said nothing. Erik wanted to pass her to enter the room. However, she stood on his way.

"No," was her strict word. "He doesn't want to see you".

"But I want to, and now get out of my way... Mother, please". He had never said anything like that to her before, but this time he had no choice. He wanted to see his father. Whatever it cost.

"Please," she begged her son. "Listen to your Mother. Just this one time".

He got his thick skull through. "No, Mother". He pushed past her and pushed the door trap down.

"Your life will change with his last breath," whispered his Mother behind him. He turned around and looked at her.

"Is that connected to the secret you were talking about?" She didn't say a word anymore because her son turned around and entered the room. When he had closed the door, he slowly stepped to the bed where the man was lying. Yes, it was the old man he had found on the street in the early hours of the morning. The man in the bed had recognized the figure who had come into the room.

"You came. I see Eva couldn't manage to stop you," he whispered. The voice sounded melancholy.

"She tried, but I always had my hard head and my strong will," said Erik Fenton and stepped to the end of the bed. Then, he hesitated a little and immediately moved to the left side, where he could better look at the man.

"Are you... Are you my father?" he asked, hesitantly.

"Yes, I am... My son,". Erik closed his eyes briefly and opened them again. These words meant so much to him. How much had he waited to hear it. He was so emotionally charged that he couldn't get a word out. He looked at the old man's face. Only now did he discover some features that were not unfamiliar to him. He saw himself in the mirror every day. Many of the small details, he had ultimately inherited from him.
"Why are you...no, why did you leave us?" he asked.

"I had my reasons."

"Does it have anything to do with a secret? Your secret?" Erik noticed how his father was frightened. His face was distorted. He must have been in incredible pain, but he couldn't make a sound over his lips. He tried to suppress the pain. 'What is wrong with him?' Erik asked himself.

The man calmed down after a few minutes. "What do you already know?" he whispered. "I tried to save you from it. I wanted to be the last of our people. If you don't leave immediately, it will hit you. Please go." It was a plea.

"What's bothering you so much, Father? I want to help you. Tell me what to do". The police instinct and curiosity in him had been aroused.

"Just go. That's all".

"No!"

"You're a stubborn man, like I was when I was a kid." The man took a short break before continuing, "Search my things". Erik Fenton stood up and walked to one of the two cupboards on the right side. He opened one. This one was empty. He also opened the other one after he had closed the first one again. His father's clothes were hanging on the clothes rail. In the bottom of the cupboard, he discovered an old rotten leather bag. "Is the leather bag there?" asked his father.

"Yes. Is that what you need?"

"Just what is inside. Put it in and take out the small leather bag". Erik did what he was told. He found the leather bag and brought it to his father. He felt something long in the bag.
'What can it be?' was his thought.

"Take it out," the father whispered. Erik opened the leather bag and grabbed it. He took out something he had never seen before. It was a small elongated cylinder. There was a hole at one end. It looked as if a matching part was missing.

'This must be iron or metal,' he thought. "What is this?" he asked.

"It's a key," came the answer.

"This cylinder is a key? It is so light. What is it made of? What kind of material is it?" The father coughed. It was the first time he heard him cough. He also spoke very softly. Erik Fenton had to listen very carefully.

"I don't know. But what you hold in your hand did not come from this world".

"Not from... this world?" Erik did not understand his father. 'Was this the secret?' Detective Fenton asked? 'No. There's got to be more.' He asked his father to "Keep talking".

"Take it with you if you want to take over my inheritance". Erik did not think long. That was the opportunity to learn something about the secret.

"I will take up your inheritance".

"I have tried everything I can to spare you. I wanted to die alone. But you put a spike in my wheel". He sighed. Then he coughed again. "I won't take longer. I feel that my life is coming to an end. Therefore, hear my words. Perhaps, you will not understand them. But when I am dead, then you will know a part of it". Erik listened to what the old man had to say.

"No matter what happens in your future…never show that you feel pain. Even if they become unbearable, never ever scream out your pain. The cylinder; the key you hold in your hand belongs to the Nameless. He will come with the warriors on a dragon and take it from you. They will seek you and find you. But they are not the only ones who will come. The others who have hunted the Nameless will come and then grace you with their presence. That could mean the end of this world. Now go, my son. Let me die alone".

Erik just looked at his father. He did not understand what he had told him. 'What or who are the warriors on a dragon? Who is the Nameless one? Who are the others?' he asked himself. He was all confused, shook his head and wanted to say something when he saw his father's pale face. It had been too much for the old man. The talking had weakened him too much. He coughed again. But this time he coughed blood. The white beard turned red. "Father!" screamed Erik. The man reared his head and sank back again. He was grasping for air. And then, the last air he had in his lungs came out of his mouth. The man was dead. Erik wanted to hurry to the door to call for a doctor when suddenly, the EEG went crazy. It beeped. The wave structure was no longer the same. Up and down, then, a straight line. The alarm went on. This mobilized the nurses and Dr. Kerren outside the door. They ran towards the room door and wanted to open it. But they could not open it. It was as if she was welded shut. Eva Fenton stood next to the hospital staff.

"My God!" she pressed her heart out full of fear. She held her clenched hands in front of her chest. "He will take over the mission," she whispered.

"The door cannot be opened!" the doctor shouted. "Get someone to break it open".

"That won't be necessary," Erik's Mother told him. "He will open it on his own when it's over".

"What's going on in there?" the doctor wanted to know. The woman in front of him was silent. "Go! Let's break it open". But their plan failed. It could not be opened. Erik also tried to open the door from the inside. But the door could not be opened. He heard the voices in front of the door, which also tried to open it. Inside, he heard something else. He turned around and saw his father lying on the bed. That was nothing unusual. Nevertheless, something had changed in this room. At first, he felt a soft vibration on his feet, which became stronger. The apparatuses also began to vibrate. Suddenly, sparks sprayed from the apparatuses and immediately exploded. A shower of sparks poured over the room. Erik ducked so as not to be hit by any parts. But that wasn't all. The vibration became strong and stronger. The ground trembled, as if an earthquake would take place only in this room. Erik had trouble finding a firm hold. The quake became stronger. The apparatus fell from the anchors of the frames and crashed to the ground. Erik also felt a breeze, which increased. Within a few seconds, he whistled and a wind storm raged through the room. The window burst into a thousand pieces of glass. Erik had no idea where this came from. He only knew that he was in the middle of this hurricane. Suddenly, he saw something incredible. The contours of his father's corpse shone in an eerie light. The light increased in intensity. The body was completely swallowed by the light. Then, the body reappeared. The light had formed a round mass over the body. In the mass, flashes twitched back and forth. Without warning, the bright energy mass became a lightning. This lightning sought its way to the person standing next to the door.

Erik Fenton was struck when the lightning hit his body. He screamed as this bundled energy hit him. It penetrated his body and disappeared. As the spook swiftly began, so it ended. No wind and no earthquake could be felt. What Erik didn't know was that part of this energy left the room window and disappeared in a Northern direction. Erik Fenton sucked in the air. He breathed heavily. Then he walked over the floor to bed. The bed was the only thing that hadn't moved. Everything else lay scattered and destroyed on the ground. Some wires hung from the wall where the apparatus had been before. Something hissed. It was the oxygen from the bottle that gave way. On the right side of the wall the small lamp was still shining. Erik bent down and picked up the small leather bag. He had dropped it before. He put it in his inner jacket pocket. Now he stood next to his father's body and looked at him. Earlier Erik didn't know what his father meant by the words. Warriors, dragons. Nameless and the others. But after the lightning—the enormous charge of energy had struck him and penetrated him; he saw everything much clearer. Now he knew part of the secret and it frightened him. He also understood why his father had left his Mother and him. He would have done the same in order not to endanger anyone.

A few moments had passed when he looked forward. The room door opened and the ceiling light from the corridor outside fell into the semi-dark room. Dr Kerren stood in the door frame and a nurse was standing behind him. "My God!" he whispered. "What happened here?" He saw the chaos in this room. Almost everything was destroyed. Then he looked at Detective Fenton standing next to the bed. "I hope you have a good explanation for all this," he said and pointed his finger to the floor. The man by the bed shook his head. Then he moved towards the people. When he was at the doctor's he said: "The patient, my father is dead". Then he walked past him. In the corridor, Erik saw his Mother. He ran towards her and embraced her.

"Oh, Mother. Why... why didn't I listen to you?" he whispered into her ear. She didn't say a word. She detached herself from him and her hands grabbed his face. Her warm hands covered his cheeks. She looked deep into his eyes.

"Is he...?"

"Yes. He is...dead, Mother".

She began to cry. "I want to see him. I want to see him".

"Better not, Mother". The two were interrupted by a voice. It belonged to Dr Kerren.

"Detective. If you don't answer me to what happened here, then I will have to talk to your superior".

"Do that, Dr Kerren". Then he turned back to his Mother. "Come. Let's go." Both of them walked through the corridors and left the hospital.

Chapter 13

It was already dark when the two of them stepped up to the car. He was standing on the parking lot in front of the hospital. "I will drive you home, Mother," said Erik.

"And then? What will happen now?" she said quietly and full of tears.

"I don't know. I only know that I have a part of the Nameless in me. I have taken over my father's mission".

"But you must decide what you will do in the future".

"I believe—no, I am sure that my life will change as of today and get out of the police service. It's too dangerous. I could get hurt and then what happens? I don't want to think about it". Erik opened his Mother's passenger door and let her in. Then he walked around the car and got in, too.

After a few moments, they were back on the road towards Oceanside. On Fulton Street, the detective's cell phone started beeping. He reached into the inside pocket of his jacket and pressed a button. "Yes?" he replied.

"This is James".

"Hi, James!"

"Erik, where are you? Your service would have started at eight. Now it is almost nine fifteen".

"I know, I know. Something has come up. I'm on Fulton Street now and I'm driving my Mother to Oceanside."

"Erik," said the Mother in the passenger seat. "You shouldn't talk on the phone while driving. That's dangerous". Erik hadn't heard what the colleague said because his Mother's voice had disturbed him.

"What did you say? Speak up!" he spoke into the portable thing.

"I wanted to say...". Erik didn't listen any further because he excessively shouted "Shit!" and dropped the cell phone.

A truck came right at him and flashed a light on him. Only now did he realize that he was driving on the wrong side. Because of him using the phone and hearing his Mother's voice, he had lost control of the car for a moment and it had sheared to the left. Hardly, he tore the steering wheel to the right again. He heard the wild honking of the truck driver's horn passing them. Erik stepped on the brake and let the car roll out at the roadside. The car was parked on a parking lot and Erik turned off the engine. Then, he turned to his Mother, who was sitting in her seat, white as chalk. She whispered, "My God!" and touched her heart. She breathed heavily.

"Hello, Erik... Hello? Are you still there?" The cell phone was lying in the floor of the car and James' voice sounded out. Erik lifted it up and spoke into it.

"I am still here. Listen. I'll call you back later, okay?" Then he broke the connection and turned right.

"Are you all right Mother?"

"You're still asking? We could have been dead because you didn't listen to me".

"You are right, Mother. I am sorry".

"You should be! Getting on the phone while driving is a punishable offense. As a police officer, you should know about that!" Erik was silent. What she said was right. He confessed to himself that he was completely confused. Not only because of driving, but also because of his father's death. This had taken him out of control.

"Should I get you some water?" he asked. He pointed to the small market one hundred and fifty meters further ahead.

"Yes, please". Erik got out of the car and walked towards the market. After a few minutes, he came out of the door of the market and wanted to walk to the car when he heard a loud noise.

Chapter 14

There's another victim," said the driver, who was sitting on a Yamaha 125. The bike was shiny. It was freshly cleaned.

"Looks good," said the other one, who was sitting behind the rider.

"Shut up!" said another motorcyclist sitting next to the two on his heavy Harley Davidson. "Concentrate on what's in front of you".

"Okay, alright!" said the first driver. Behind his closed helmet, his voice sounded dull. The visor he had pulled down. On the Plexiglas the city lights shimmered again. The driver was completely dressed in leather. The other, who sat behind him, was not wearing a helmet. Only dark jeans, a shirt that was open to the middle and a leather vest. Around the neck, some necklaces strummed. The long hair he wore open and his face looked mean and dangerous. The other rider on the Harley said, "Here we go". The guy on the Yamaha started the engine. He howled and accelerated.

Chapter 15

Helen Turner was at the ATM. She wore a dark blue skirt and a matching jacket. The shoes also looked dark blue. The legs were wrapped in beautiful transparent stockings. "How annoying," she murmured. That evening, she had invited an old friend to her home and of course forgot this date. She wanted some fine dining and talk to her friend about the old times. Just spend a nice evening together. She was looking forward to it. The girlfriend would come at ten o'clock. Now it was half past nine. She only had half an hour left. That's why she hurried. She rummaged around in her handbag. 'Where is the darn card? Oh, it's to...ah, there it is,' she thought. There was such a mess in the handbag that she almost didn't find the card. The twenty-eight-year-old woman put the card into the ATM. Then she entered her code and the money came out. The tin machine spat out 200 US dollars. She hastily put the money away in her handbag, took the card out of the slot of the machine and turned right. Fifty yards down the road was Jerry's little market. She knew the owner because she often bought from him. She stepped on it when she heard a noise coming closer.

Chapter 16

From the right side of the road, a Yamaha drove to the left side. It found its way between the parking cars and immediately the tires touched the pavement. The driver now drove on the sidewalk in the direction of the woman.

"Stand by", the driver spoke to the man behind him. He patted him on the shoulder. The few people who were now on the sidewalk saw the bike coming at them. They tried to get to safety so as not to be run over. The only one who heard the sound, but did not look back, was Helen Turner. That was a mistake she would regret. From now on, everything went very fast. "Step on the gas!" shouted the guy in the back seat. The driver accelerated. He drove as fast as he could towards the woman. She heard the engine behind her. She turned her head back and saw the bike coming towards her. It was a moment of shock she went through. She did not know how to react. In her right hand, she held her handbag.

The guy with both hands-free bent briefly to the left and grabbed the bag. He grabbed it, held it tight and at the same time shot his arm forward. With his elbow, he hit the woman at the shoulder. The blow was so violent that she swayed and went down to the left. She hit the ground with her knees. Her stockings tore, and she scraped the skin on her knees. She screamed. It wasn't the pain she felt for a moment, but that she taken by surprise in the worst way possible. "I got it," the guy hissed. "Go!". But they didn't get far.

Chapter 17

Erik Fenton saw a motorcycle riding on the sidewalk. There were two guys sitting on it. The rider on the bike approached a woman. The guy behind the rider bent to the left and grabbed the woman's handbag. It was also hit by him and knocked to the ground. The motorbike was driving towards him. He dropped the bag with the bottle of water on the floor. Since it was a pet bottle, it did not break when it hit the ground. Erik acted. The motorcycle was now at its height. With a jump forward, he hit the bike with his legs in half. It began to shake. The rider could no longer keep the bike under control and fell to the ground. Erik, who was lying on the ground for a moment from the impact, was already on his feet again and watched what happened. The machine slipped with sparks over the ground until it stopped. It would never drive again, as it looked. The two men on the motorcycle rolled over the ground. The rider had the helmet on. It protected him from the impact with a light mast.

Only a "Ping!" was heard when he hit his head. The man remained lying because he had fallen into a deep impotence. The helmet had saved his life. The other lost the handbag and rolled over the floor as well. He crashed into a parking car. He felt little pain because he was a tough guy. He rubbed his palms and a little of the right half of his face. He cursed "Shit!". He already wanted to get up when he heard footsteps. Nevertheless, he straightened up and already he felt two hands. It was Detective Fenton's hands.

He spoke, "Not so fast, my friend," and pushed him against the car. "Nice legs wide and hands behind you". The detective's hands touched the man's body. He felt something hard in the waistband.

"Look at that. What have we got here?" he said and pulled out a gun. "I hope you have a gun license for that".

"Fuck me!" the guy spat with a foreign accent.

"Oh, you'd like that". After a few seconds, the handcuffs clicked around the guy's joints. Erik read his right hand to him and pushed the guy in front of him. Both of them stepped back to the market. Erik saw from a distance that the woman who had fallen to the ground was being helped. She was already on her feet again. Someone had brought her handbag back to her. From a distance, everyone heard the sirens. Someone had called the cops. After a few moments, they were there and took the purse thief into custody.

"Go down with the turnip," spoke a cop as he pressed the man's head down, and he got in the back.

Before the door was closed, he called out. "Hey, you!". He meant the detective who had arrested him. Erik turned around and looked at the man.
He said, "What now, my friend?"

"You'll be sorry for that. I promise you".

"Oh, really?" said Erik. The guy had stretched his head out too far. Erik Fenton did not miss this opportunity. He kicked with his foot. The target was the back door of the car. It closed at lightning speed. Unfortunately, the guy's head was in the way. He howled as the door hit his face, or nose, respectively.

He cried out, "My nose! He broke my nose!" He was bleeding. The precious juice flowed over his mouth and spread over his shirt and chest.

"Detective," said one of the cops. "Do you have to?"

"I don't like being threatened. By the way, did you see anything?"

"No, not us, but the people standing here. If the captain finds out, all hell will break loose".

"It's all right," said Erik. "Take him away. I don't want to see these guys anymore".

"Okay". The two cops left after picking up the other guy from the sidewalk. The machine stopped until someone from another department came to take it away. Erik Fenton walked towards the woman. When he was with her, he spoke to her.

"Everything is fine now. Are you all right?" The woman looked at him and nodded.

"Should I call you an ambulance if you're in pain?"

"No, no. Except for a few abrasions on my knees, I'm fine," she said.

"Would you like to file charges against them?" She was frightened.

"Against them? I'm not crazy. If I do, they'll attack me sooner or later".

"I understand your fear. But if you don't, these two will get out of the cell as soon as possible. All that does not have to happen because it's up to you. So? How will you decide?"

She thought about it. "Do you think the legal system works?"

"As a rule, it does, but there may be exceptions".

"Aha! There, you said so yourself. It's better if I don't".

"Well, it's your decision. But I will do it for you. I'll put these two under lock and key if it calms you down. Do you agree?" She shrugged her shoulders and didn't say a word. She already wanted to say goodbye to the man when everyone heard a noise. An engine was started. Across the street was a Harley Davidson. The driver on the seat turned the throttle so the engine howled. Then the rider stepped on the gas. He slowly drove past the onlookers and looked over at the two people paying attention to him. He turned the throttle more down and accelerated the bike. Soon he was out of sight of the people.
"Hmm. Guess the rider was one of the other two" Erik Fenton muttered.

The woman had heard him. "Do you really think so?"

"Everything is possible".

"Then, he saw us and will remember what happened". Erik made no comment. What the woman said was right. He thought, 'She's sharp-witted'. Although he had only seen her for the first time today, he had the feeling that he had known her for some time. He liked her very much and what he liked about her was that she saw things in the right light. The woman gave him her hand.

"What was your name again?" she asked. "I didn't get it".

"Oh, excuse me. I forgot to mention myself. My name is Fenton. Erik Fenton".

"Well then, Mr. Fenton. Thank you so much for helping me get my bag back".

"It's my job".

"Are you a cop?"

"Just a simple detective." He murmured out the last word, "Still..."

She heard it and asked, "Why?"

He waved off. "Not important".

"Well, then. Goodbye, Detective Fenton". She turned around and walked towards the market where she wanted to shop.

He called out "Wait!" after her. "What's your name, Miss?"

"Helen Turner," she quickly replied, and entered the market after a few steps. Erik also stepped up to the market, picked up his mineral bottle that was lying on the floor, and then ran back to his car. His mother had been waiting for him.

"You were long gone. What was going on up there?" she asked when he got in and handed her the mineral bottle.

He said "Oh, nothing," so as not to worry his mother. She had been through enough in the last hours. The Mother emptied the water into a paper cup that Erik had brought along and drank the cool water. She felt much better than before. Erik started the car and the two went to Oceanside.

Chapter 18

It was 2:30 in the morning. Erik Fenton was on his way to Brooklyn again with his VW Golf. At some point, his portable mobile phone beeped. Despite the exhaustion, he lost weight. He said, "Yes," briefly into the little thing.

"Hello, Erik. It's me," he heard the other one on the line.

"Hello, James. What's up?".

"The Captain showed up here. He wants to see you."

"Do you know what he wants?"

"I don't know, but he's pissed off. It's better if you show up here as soon as possible".

"Yes, yes. I'll be in Brooklyn soon anyway. Just stall him for me. Okay?"

"All right," James said, breaking the connection. Erik also did this and threw his cell phone on the side seat. He thought he knew why the captain wanted to talk to him. After about half an hour, he stopped his car in front of the Police District West. After entering the building, he walked up the stairs on the right. There was a single hall at the top and tables and chairs were everywhere. Individual rooms, such as, cells, interrogation rooms, and others were available for the working police officers. At this late hour, the devil was loose here. Some cops brought a screaming horde of prostitutes into a closed room. Another cop led a handcuffed man past Erik Fenton. 'A madhouse as always,' Erik thought as he stepped on his desk.

The Captain's office was two desks away. Despite the closed door, the Captain looked out into the hall as the wall was made of glass. He discovered Erik Fenton's arrival. Then, he got up from his chair and walked to the door. He opened it and called through the room. "Detective Fenton. Please come to my office".

'Oh... he's in a mood again,' Erik thought and twisted his eyes. He stepped towards the office. His eyes fell on the other employees who were looking after him. Everybody was thinking the same thing right now. Nobody wanted to be in his skin when he was angry. The captain stood behind his desk and expected his assistant to come into the door. 'How many times had I been in this office?' he thought. The boss's name was written in black letters on the glass door. Captain Tom Stone.

"Close the door," he spoke with a voice that promised nothing good. Erik did this and took a step toward his superior.

With a friendly voice, he spoke to him. "Captain, what are you doing here at this hour?"

The man behind the desk took a deep breath. His face turned red and redder until he exploded. "What am I doing here?!" he yelled at him. His voice sounded like a thunderclap. All the staff on the other side of the office stopped working and listened to the Captain's lovely voice. "Damn!" he cursed. "Why do you think I'm here?"

Erik shrugged his shoulders. "Because you couldn't sleep?"

"Exactly, you joker." He took a deep breath. "Damn it! What was going on in the hospital?" he wanted to know.

"Oh, that?"

"Yes, exactly that. How would you feel if the phone rang in the middle of the night and the mayor took you out of your sleep?"

"I don't know?"

"You don't know? But one thing you know, for sure, is that you have smashed the furniture in a room". There was a short break before the captain continued. "What were you thinking?!"

"Who told you?"

"A Dr. Kerren called the mayor and complained. So! Why did you go into the room of an injured bum and destroy the equipment?"

Erik Fenton lowered his head until he raised his head again and looked at the captain with watery eyes.

"What's the matter with you?" asked the supervisor and saw the eyes of his employee.

Erik cleared his throat until he said something. "This dead man, whom you called a bum, was my father!"

That was a surprise and a little shock for the Captain. He sat down on his chair and leaned back. "Your father?" he whispered.

"Yes. I never saw him. I thought back when I was little that he had died. But this was not true. I heard it a few hours ago from my Mother. I wanted to see him and went to the hospital. When I finally went to see him, he passed away."

"I give you my condolences. I'm sorry about your father," the captain said. "But the question is still present. Why did you make the room like that?"

"I can't tell you that".

"And why not?"

"You wouldn't believe me anyways".
"Oh. I wouldn't understand it". The man in the armchair leaned forward and laid his palms on the desk.

"If that's the case, then I have no choice but to suspend you from your duty until you tell me". Erik had a presentiment that this would happen. He reached into his inner jacket pocket and took out his ID without saying a word. He put it on the desk. He also took his service weapon from the holder hidden under his jacket, unlocked it and placed it next to his ID.

"I swore this to myself when I came out of my father's room. You didn't even have to tell me, Captain. I want to officially get out of the police service and try to start a new life".

"What!? You're not serious, are you?"

"Dead serious. Those," he pointed to the two things on the desk, "are the proof. I will bury my father soon and then you will not see me again". He turned around and wanted to leave.

"Wait a moment!" said the Captain. "What's with this sudden change? Why are you doing everything so fast and incomprehensible?"

"I cannot tell you. But there's one thing you should know. If it should hit me, then may God have mercy upon us".

With these words, he walked out of the office and left the house. Captain Tom Stone sat in his chair and thought about what his ex-employee had said. 'I didn't know Erik like that. Something is wrong. There must be something he's not telling me clearly,' was his thought.

He didn't think long and called two of his people into the office. The two detectives entered the office. "What is it?" one asked.

"Listen up. I'll only say it once and it will stay between us. Do I have your approval?" The two nodded even though they didn't know what the Captain wanted from them. "A few hours ago, Erik Fenton's father died. After the funeral, I assume he will be gone in the next few days, and you will take over a task. Everything you're working at the moment, you put it back or pass it on to your colleagues. From the day after the funeral, you will shadow him. Every hour of the day and night. If you need help, turn to me".

"Why do all this, Captain?"

"I suspect there is something wrong with Erik Fenton. You will shadow him until I think it is necessary to release you from this task. That will be all. You can go".

"Yes, Sir," they commented and left the office.

"Hopefully, I'm doing the right thing," Tom Stone said whispering to himself.

Chapter 19

Monday morning on the Holy Cross Cemetery in Brooklyn. Eva and Erik Fenton stood in front of the grave. This cemetery was near Erik Fenton's apartment. So, he could always go to his father's grave. The two family members were not the only ones in the cemetery. Besides the priest, who had spoken some comforting words for the deceased, there were also innumerable bums that had appeared at the grave, to pay their last honor to the dead one. Smithy was also there. The bum smelled penetrating like the others. Captain Tom Stone had also appeared. He stayed in the background and didn't want to disturb his former employee. When the coffin was let into the depth, Eva Fenton stood as the first before the grave and lifted a little earth. She held the earth in her right hand and slowly let it trickle through her fingers. She fell on the coffin and spread out over the wood. She murmured in tears "Rest in peace". Then she turned left, where her son stood. He also lifted the earth and let it fall into the grave.

'I am the last one to keep your secret' he thought.

Now he turned around and held his mother by the arm. The two of them walked across the meadow to the cart, which was nearby. Erik took a quick look over his shoulder and saw the bums, the homeless, standing at the grave. They also threw a piece of earth into the grave. Erik turned his head again and helped his mother get in. He wanted to bring them back to Oceanside and also to get away from this cemetery. Only one voice stopped him for a short moment. It was the captain who had followed them and approached him.

"Mr. Fenton. One moment, please".

"Yes, what is it?"
"I want to offer my condolences to you and your mother". He reached out his hand, which Erik grasped, and returned the handshake.

"If you have something on your mind, let me know".

"Thank you" pressed Erik out.

They both wanted to say goodbye when the captain said something else.

"I'm sorry to have to say this now, but do you remember the night before you came to my office?"

"Yes, what about it?"

"I have been informed that you have managed to arrest two men. These two belong to one of the dangerous motorcycle gangs that have been making the roads unsafe for a long time. The one you smashed his nose into, which of course I didn't see, is a wanted criminal. His account includes countless thefts, burglaries and even some sadistic murders. His name is Kalish".

"That's strange name for an American," said Erik.

"He's Ami. A man from the Middle East. One who has already been through several acts of terrorism. This is the best catch in a long time for the police authorities. That is their merit. Thank you".

"I hope he will go behind bars for a long time".

"He will. If not, I hope on the electric chair. But unfortunately, something failed with this precious freight".

"What happened?"

"The prisoner transporter was intercepted. Someone freed this criminal from the car and shot the two guards and then killed them. He's at large again. I mobilized all police forces and ordered a search, unfortunately without success. The guy is submerged".

Erik understood. "When I made the arrest, another guy drove past us on a Harley Davidson. I suspect that he informed his accomplices and that this liberation operation took place," said Fenton.

The Captain said, "This may well be the case".

Maybe Erik would meet this guy again. He decided to be vigilant. The two spoke a little before they parted ways. They left the cemetery and drove off in different directions.

Chapter 20

One day later. It was afternoon when the Captain's door was knocked, and he opened it up immediately. A man entered. He spoke, "Captain".

"What is it, Thompson?"

"It's about the order you gave Ferris and me."

"Yes. What about it?"

"Well. Fenton is gone".

"What do you mean he's gone?" The captain stood up behind the desk and surrounded him. "Where did he go?"

"We lost him. The only thing we know is that he took flight at 8:25 to Rome. There, he rented a car and headed somewhere to Saranac Lake. We learned that from the car rental company".

"Oh," the captain said. "Then I know where he is at the moment".

"You know?"

"Yes. He went to his friend who lives in the wilderness. As of the moment, Fenton is taking his fishing rod and landing some big fish. Should we fly there and shadow him?"

"No, that's not necessary. Go on about your work. But you should check the flights, the car rentals, and the trains of Rome every day if the name Fenton appears on any list. I just want to know where he is at every moment".

"Okay," Thompson said and left the office.

Chapter 21

Month of June. It was the 28th when Detective Thompson entered the Captain's office. "Captain. Fenton is back. He came from Rome on 20:00".

"Good. Where is he now?" The captain was holding some documents in his hands. He put them on the desk.

"Fenton is at home. Ferris called and reported".

"Okay. Now it's on again. You continue to shadow him, but keep your distance. He should not notice anything".

Detective Thompson nodded and left the office.

Chapter 22

Erik Fenton was back in New York. 'Finally, back home,' he thought as he entered his small apartment. He had been away for almost a month and a half. He spoke "Phew!" to himself. "Here it stinks of stale air". He hurried to the window and opened it. But the better air didn't come in from outside either. More came from the exhaust fumes of the cars than the fresh air. He immediately missed the fine and clean air from the woods where he was recently. He couldn't always stay there, because he had an apartment that he had to pay for. Erik would not have money for the rest of his life. Therefore, he had to come back. He had definitely quit his job as a detective and now he devoted himself to a new task. Although he knew too little about this task and the pay was not as high as a detective, he would learn. He had found work with Jerry Hanson, the owner of the small market on Fulton Street. He was responsible for ordering and stocking the goods on the shelves. There was also something else. Since he knew the streets well, he could also make some home deliveries. The fact that he accepted this work did not bother him. On the contrary, he could collect some generous tips from the recipients. On the 1st of July, the time had come. Until then, he still had time to settle in and dream of the past days. Of course, he also visited his Mother in between.

Chapter 23

Month of August. Sunday. Today, Erik Fenton got freedom. He owed it to his boss Jerry Hanson. Erik had settled in well to his new job. Thanks to him, sales had also skyrocketed. This was due to the fact that he was able to handle home deliveries promptly and reliably. He had to say that he liked this work. He felt comfortable in the small market. That was certainly due to the fact that a certain Helen Turner appeared from time to time. In the beginning, she was surprised when she saw him working there. The two greeted each other, although the question of why he quit his job as a detective was on her lips, she didn't ask him. She was sure that one day he would tell her. Days passed. By the time they met, the two found each other more and more sympathetically. The simple greetings turned into several short conversations. She liked this Erik Fenton. Even though she was eleven years younger, he felt more than sympathy for her. Today was the weekend. He wanted to meet her in Flushing Meadow in Corona Park, Queens. Since she was already there, he knew because she had been with a friend who lived nearby. They spent the whole afternoon together, stretching until evening. It was about half past nine when they wanted to say goodbye.

"You're sure you want to stay with your girl friend?" he asked. They had offered themselves the 'You' nickname this afternoon.

"Yes. I will stay with her and go straight to work tomorrow morning".

"Well then," he said. He accompanied her to the girl friend's apartment. In front of the front door, they said goodbye.

"I wish you a good night and see you tomorrow evening?"

She nodded. "Thank you for this wonderful day," she said quietly. Then, she gave him a kiss on the cheek and entered the house entrance. As the door closed, she climbed up the stairs to the first floor. She entered the apartment and turned on the lights. The girl friend wasn't there yet. She wanted to come home later. Erik saw from downstairs that the light in the living room went on and moved away from the house. He did not see that he was being watched by Detective Ferris. Neither did the figure on the motorcycle lurking around a corner.

Chapter 24

The man on the motorcycle reached into the inside pocket of his leather jacket and pulled out a cell phone. By pressing a button on the device, he activated a phone number in his contacts. A connection was established. He whispered, "Yes," in order to remain unnoticed. "I'm at 139th Street in Queens. I found the woman. The man who put a spoke in our wheel at the time is also here. He is now heading towards Flushing Meadow Park. I suspect he wants to cross it and come out on Grand Central".

"Okay," said the voice at the other end. "Eight other men and Me are nearby. I'll send two of them to you. The others will go to the park where we will wait for the guy. You'll follow when the other two have the wife".

That was the end of the conversation.

Chapter 25

Detective Ferris started the car and slowly followed Erik Fenton. He remained at a safe distance without being seen. He saw Fenton walking towards Flushing Meadow Park. He could not follow him in the car. That's why he had to take another path. He accelerated the car and drove through some streets to get to the other side of the park. There he wanted to hit Fenton again. He did not know that he was being watched by the motorcyclist who had waited next to the house.

Chapter 26

Now that was a beautiful day,' Erik thought as he walked through the park. In his mind, the name Helen Turner had appeared again and again. He had to admit to himself that he felt a lot for this woman. Yes, he was sure to love her. But he had doubts. Was it really sensible to get involved in a relationship now? Now that he had a secret inside him? He was in a dilemma. Should he confess to her what's depressing him? Maybe she would understand, like his Mother did with his Father back then. If not, what then? With mixed feelings, he walked through the small paths of the park until he came to the big square. Behind the concrete square came again the lawn and the sidewalks. From somewhere, he heard police sirens disappearing again. It was about 22:50 when he stood on the square. That was a few seconds ago when he had looked at his watch. On this square, there were no street lights illuminating the surroundings like on the sidewalks. That's why he moved faster. He knew that sometimes death could lurk in the darkness. As soon as he was in the middle of the square, something happened. As if bitten by a snake, he stopped when a sea of lights lit up before his eyes. He held his right hand in front of his eyes so as not to be blinded anymore. "Hey!" he shouted. "What are you doing?"

Someone had turned on some lamps to scare him. He heard nothing. No one gave him an answer. Only a nasty giggle came from the direction of the lights. Then a hell raged into that night's rest. Beside the lights, engines were ignited. It was motorcycles that caused this noise. Now Erik understood what those lights were. Then the headlights moved and movement came into the heavy machines. The lights danced left and right past Erik. He vaguely recognized the contours of the motorcyclists passing him. Despite the noise he could count seven riders. They rode in circles around him and made the engines howl.

"Damn it. What game is being played here?" cursed and screamed Erik into the noise. He firmly believed that nobody could hear him.

The circle of motorcycles tightened. Erik put his hand under the jacket, as he always did, but he found nothing. He hadn't carried a gun ever since he left the police service. This annoyed him even more when he reached out his hand into the void. 'Shit!' he thought, spinning like a motorcycle in a circle. Subsequently, he could at least keep them a little under control. The roar had become louder and in between, he heard something strange. Something that didn't match the motorcycles. It was something hard, dangerous and not unique. Each of the motorcyclist had it in his hand. It was thick metal chains, and they swung back and forth. A motorcyclist now drove close to Erik and swung the chain over his head. Then he struck him with it. Erik, who hadn't been paying attention, felt the chain. It hit his back. He groaned as he felt the blow. The back burned and hurt after the chain hit him. He staggered forward like a drunk.

The next driver came and caught him on his knees. The blow brought Erik to his knees. He screamed inside. He had to, because he was not allowed to scream out his pain. Subsequently, he pressed his lips together. That was also better, because the next blow at the back of his head robbed him of his consciousness. He tilted forward and hit the asphalt with his face. Motionless, he remained lying on the ground.

The motorcyclists stopped their machines and switched off the engines. Silence returned. But this silence was interrupted when one of the riders got off a machine and approached the unconscious man. With his legs apart, he stood in front of Erik and giggled. "The world is indeed small," he said. "I was hardly away for a short time, and yet we meet again." The man was no less than Kalish. The man who Erik arrested at that time. "This time, you fucking cop, I'm the winner".

The guy turned around and spoke to the motorists. "Call Rick. He and the other two should come with the car, load up this bull and bring him into the hall".

"Not necessary", said the man. "They're coming already". A car drove without lights down the small street that led to the square. Behind the dark van a motorbike followed. The two vehicles stopped in front of the motorcyclist and turned off the engines. The doors of the car opened and two men got out. They belonged to the gang. "And?" Kalish said, walking towards the two. "Do you have the woman?"

One guy bobbed his thumb backwards. "She was a little reluctant when we entered the apartment, but Rick's chin hook worked. She lies in the back and is sleeping like a marmot".

"Well done," praised Kalish. "Then you can pick up this son of a bitch here and lie him down with her".

"Okay," said the guy. The two of them lifted Erik Fenton up and carried him to the car. They pushed the side door to the side and threw him into the car. There he lay him next to an unconscious Helen Turner. The door closed again. Kalish stepped on the one motorcyclist.

"Was there trouble?" he asked.

"I don't know yet whether it still exists".

"What do you mean by that?"

"When I called you, a car drove away from the house shortly afterwards. It was possible that a cop or a private detective was also on the way to shadow the guy in the car".

"Hmm..." Kalish scratched his cheek and thought.

"Okay. Let's not take any chances. Let's split up. Some of them drive straight to the hall. The others take a detour via the 295th. You," he said the two who drove the van "You drive up the 495th. Bend into the 678th and then before Whitestone, go to the hall. All right?" The drivers nodded. "Then go". He also got on his bike, started it and followed the others. On the road, they separated. Everyone knew what to do.

Chapter 27

On the dark side of the road, Detective Ferris sat in the car waiting for Erik Fenton to come out of the park. But he didn't show up. Instead, a small dark van turned into the narrow road that led straight into the park. A motorbike also drove behind the car. Ferris thought, 'There is something wrong'. He stayed in the car and waited. 'At some point, the car will come out again'. After a few minutes, it came out, but he was not alone. A horde of motorcyclists drove behind him. On the road, they separated. Ferris didn't know what to do. Should he follow the one motorcyclist or the other? "Shit!" he cursed before himself and hammered with the left fist on the steering wheel. Then, he decided. The small van was more important. He wanted to follow it at a safe distance. He started the van and accelerated.

Chapter 28

The journey of the small van ended in Riverside. It was the Queens district. The area was called Whitestone and lay on the East River. The van drove between some uninhabited houses and stopped in front of a house. It was a small warehouse. It used as a warehouse for goods that were transported by ship across the East River. The rented company had filed for bankruptcy years ago because it no longer made a profit. Today nobody cared for the hall anymore. The people who lost their jobs left the area. One day, a gang of motorcyclists appeared and took possession of the hall and part of the houses. The warehouse stood behind the houses and is unseen from the front or from the street. There was an iron double door leading into the hall. There were also countless windows above the door and along the wall. These were placed at a height so that no one could look in from the outside. Except that this one had a ladder. In front of the warehouse, there were about twenty motorcycles in a row. The two drivers of the van got out. One went to the door and knocked his mark on the metal. Immediately, the door opened on one side and two men stepped out. They went to the van and helped carry the two unconscious men inside the warehouse. They handled the woman better than Erik Fenton. The two men dragged him across the floor. Then, one closed the door behind him after the others were inside.

Chapter 29

Detective Ferris stopped his car in the street. He saw the dark van slowly disappear behind the block of flats. He saw a red-light fade in briefly, reflected on the wall of the house. 'Those were the brake lights. Subsequently, here is the hiding place of this gang,' he thought and reached for the radio. "Here is car 20. Central, please come," he said into the technical device.

The answer came immediately. "Here Central. What is it, car 20?"

"This is Jack Ferris. Give me Detective Thompson".

"One moment, please."

It cracked on the line. A few moments after, he heard Thompson's voice. "Yes?"

"It's me. There is trouble".

"Ferris. Where are you and why is there trouble?" he asked.

"I followed Fenton. He went to Flushing Meadow Park and didn't come out again. Someone else showed up."

"Who is it? Don't make it so exciting".

"As I said, Fenton wasn't there, but a motorcycle gang".

"What!?"

"You heard it right. The guys showed up from the park. Likewise, a small dark van. I followed them and now stand next to the 152nd in Queens. The road leads into 6th Street in Riverside near Whitestone. The gang certainly has Fenton. I need reinforcements and tell the Captain. Come as fast as you can. Ferris out!" Ferris put the radio in the holder and waited for the people from the Brooklyn Police District.

Chapter 30

Thompson told the captain what he had learned from Ferris. "All available men must hurry. We will smoke out the rat's nest and free Fenton," Tom Stone shouted to the crowd. In no time, the Police District was even more hectic than usual. The captain gave some instructions and left the house, along with the other cops.

Chapter 31

Erik Fenton emerged from unconsciousness. Dazed, he shook his head. He grumbled and hurt. He felt a pull on his back and legs. Fenton tasted something sticky on his lips and in his mouth. It was blood. He had hit the ground in the park on his nose. The blood in his face had almost dried up. Erik wanted to move, but something held him back. He breathed deeply until his eyes got used to the light. Again, he shook his head and blinked his eyes. Only now did he recognize something. From the ceiling, a light bulb lit up only a part of where he was. He noticed that he was sitting on a chair. His legs were tied to the legs of the chair, so, were his hands. His hands were tied to the front of the side rests with strong ropes. Pressure was also felt on his upper body. There he was also tied up. The memory of his capture came again. 'The guys in the park must have kidnapped me,' he thought. But he did not see any of these motorcyclists. That's why he tried to free himself.

"I wouldn't try it if I were you," spoke a voice from the dark.

"Who's there?!" Erik shouted into the dark.

"Someone you know," came the answer with a broken accent. Suddenly, a figure emerged from the darkness and stepped into the light. Now Erik recognized who had spoken. It was the one he had arrested almost two and a half months ago. He still looked the same. Around his neck he wore his chains that clashed against each other and his long hair open. On the right half of his face, some stains were still visible from the accident, and his nose was a little swollen. The guy who stood two meters in front of him looked viciously at him. "I see that you still remember me". Fenton didn't speak a word. He knew what his former captain had said at the cemetery.

'Why is this terrorist here and not in jail?' he thought.

"Well... My friend, you must be surprised to see me here".

"Don't call me your friend. I can do without such friends".

Kalish just looked at him and his eyes flashed dangerously. "You will be sorry for what you did to me," he whispered to Erik. He snapped his finger and the hall lit up. There wasn't much light, but it was enough to overlook the hall. Erik swallowed, because he didn't like what he saw. Earlier, he hadn't seen anyone in the darkness. But now?

Behind Kalish, there were about twenty men in motorbike crevasses, looking viciously at Erik Fenton. Some of them wore their motorcycle glasses on their noses and the light of the few light bulbs reflected from the ceiling. Behind the men lay some boxes. What he saw were two men among the others, who somehow didn't fit. At this distance, he could not see their faces. His gaze wandered around again. There was a wooden door to Kalish's right and one to his left. But it was made of iron. That is as much as he could see.

"Surprised?" Kalish asked. Erik didn't speak a word. "Of course, you are. I see it in your eyes. But what I have to offer you now will throw you straight out of your socks".

"What?"

"Look behind you". He raised his arm and pointed with his index finger behind him. Erik tried to turn his head but failed.

"I cannot turn my head. You can see that," said Erik angrily.

"I can help you with that". Kalish turned around and called into the rows of motorbikes. "Petit". There was movement in the rows. A small alleyway developed and made room for the one who was called. Erik knew what Petite meant. But the term small was not even close enough to the giant that came to him. He was at least two heads bigger and twice as wide in the shoulders. "Petit doesn't say much, but he does everything I tell him," Kalish whispered to his prisoner. A mountain of muscles came up to Erik and stopped in front of him. Then he grabbed the chair with Erik on it and turned it 180 degrees. What Erik got to see was a shock to him. Helen Turner also sat on a chair and she was tied too. On her cheeks, tears ran down. They gathered under her chin and fell on her lap. She didn't say a word. "Helen," Erik whispered. She just looked at him. Erik noticed someplace was red on her face, as if someone had hit her.

"Erik," she sobbed, "I am scared," she said these three words in a whisper.

"You don't need to. I am with you," he tried to calm her down, although it was hopeless. Who could know that Helen and he were here? Nobody!

"How long have we been here?" he asked.

"I don't know. You were unconscious for a long time. But not me. When I woke up, the man there," she referred to Kalish, "told me that I should be silent until you wake up. I did not. I screamed. But he silenced me. He hit me. It hurts". She cried again.

"How touching," Kalish said behind Erik's back.

"You damn pig!" screamed Erik and tried to free himself. He shook the chair like a savage. But Petit forcefully calmed him down. He turned the chair around again and slapped Erik. Erik felt this slap in the face like a hammer blow. 'If he caught me with his fist, I'd be a goner,' he thought and kept his mouth shut.

"Did the loud and wriggling bundle of a baby calm down?" Kalish asked. Erik was silent. But he promised this guy one thing. If he came out of this situation alive, he would chase him to the end of the world. Petit walked past the chair and moved to the right. Next to the iron door stood a table that Erik hadn't noticed before. Petit lifted it up and put it behind Kalish, who was still standing two meters in front of Erik. There he put it down. Erik couldn't see anything on the table because this long-haired guy was standing in front of him. "You must have a lot of questions about why you're here," Kalish began.

"Yes. What do you want from us?"

"I like this guy!" he laughed, mockingly. "I want to have some fun and you surely want to know why I am here".

"Yes".

"Look here". Kalish turned around and picked something up from the table. It was a newspaper. Erik couldn't read the date because he didn't care. He already knew it. Rather, the bold lines were on the front page:

SPECTACULAR ESCAPE FROM PRISONER TRANSPORT

He couldn't read the small print below because Kalish put the newspaper away again. "I couldn't read the small letters," said Erik Fenton. "I'm sure it says there that you steal the handbag from helpless women".

"You piece of shit! You don't know who I am, do you? I am the leader of this gang".

"How pathetic you are. A leader that steals handbags. How deep you must have sunk".

"I wanted to try it out. Otherwise, the other members would do that".

"Which also failed. How's your nose?"

Kalish was dangerous and unpredictable. His outburst of rage showed that. He slapped Erik's hand in the face. Then he calmed down again and continued speaking calmly. "You arrested me, but I didn't go to jail".

"The other motorcyclist made sure of that, didn't he?"

"Yes. That was a thing. I had friends and helpers who supported me. The transport was easy to crack, but at the guards, we had to grit our teeth. The two guards died. The escape was successful and until today nobody has caught us. Subsequently, you see that we are a unit that nobody can overcome so easily". Kalish felt confident and so convinced of himself. His words were euphorically spoken, as if he could overcome everything and everyone.

"What I see are criminals who do not shy away from anything," said Erik. He answered nothing to that remark.

He just asked, "Was that all you wanted to know?"

"No. I want to know who they are. The two, I mean, who don't suit you".

"Oh those? They were on the transport. They were arrested before me. I took them with me when I broke out. You never know when you need help".

"What are their names?"

Kalish waved them to him. When they were with him, Erik looked at them. These faces looked familiar to him. He had surely seen them in one of the case files before. But what were their names? When he heard it from Kalish, his face changed. "These are Max Conti and Phil Travis".

"Untie me," raved Erik.

"Why?"

"I will kill them!" Erik cursed and tried to free himself.

"Why so aggressive?"

Fenton didn't answer the question. Instead, he asked one of the two. "Which of you two hit the man on the street the night you went into the light pole?" Neither of them answered.

"Come on, you sons of bitches!"

"Why should they?" Kalish asked.

"Why do I want to know? Because it's their fault that I'm here now. It is also their fault that I could arrest you".

Kalish threw his head back. His long hair fell down, and he was slightly sweating, which shone on the ceiling light. He shouted, "Answer!" dangerously. "Tell the truth. I want to know every single detail". Both of them became pale.

Travis, to the left of Conti, moved his mouth to the side and whispered into his ear, "Shit! Now we are on dirty bricks".

"Shut the fuck up," said Conti whispering. "Is it my fault you couldn't drive properly?"

"So? What is it? Talk!" Kalish had raised his voice.

"If they can't answer, I'll tell you. The night before, one of them shot a guard in the Terminal Market". That's what Erik Fenton learned from the homicide squad.

"I know that already. That was Conti. He told me," Kalish said. "Keep talking".

"When they escaped, they caused an accident in which a man was hit. That man was my father. When I was in the hospital, he died of his injuries. My Mother was also there. When I drove her home, I happened to come to Fulton Street. My Mother asked for water because it was warm in the car. Subsequently, I stopped in front of the market and got her a small bottle of water. It was really a coincidence that you, of all people, showed up," he said to Kalish, "And wanted to steal the handbag from the woman behind me. Technically, you see that you owe everything to the two of them". Kalish's eyes flashed dangerously as he looked at them. Anger came up in him. The two saw their skins swimming away.

"I told you it was a mistake to go with him," Conti whispered.

"Okay, what do you suggest?" Travis quietly returned.

"Off through the middle. The door on your right isn't closed".

"Then let's go". The two of them jumped to the right from a standing position and wanted to go to the door but they hadn't noticed Petit. He had stepped behind them and slowly moved to the door. Somehow, he had smelled that the two would do something. Like a rock, he suddenly stood in front of the door and stopped both of them. The two paws held Travis and Conti. There was no escape. There was movement in the pack of motorcyclist. They rushed to Petit and helped him hold the two.

"You traitors! You wanted to run away and even betray our hiding place," Kalish said. "You will be sorry for that. Go! Tie them up. I'll judge you later when I'm done with this cop here". Both of them were brought to the crates and tied up with ropes. Like a pile of misery, they sat there on the floor waiting for their punishment. "So," Kalish spoke and dedicated himself to the cop. "Do you want to know anything else before you die?" Erik shook his head. "That's good because now I want to let off some steam".

Chapter 32

With blue lights, the cops chased towards the district Queens. Hoping not to come too late. 'I knew I wasn't wrong to have Fenton watched,' Tom Stone thought. During the trip, he looked at his watch. "Damn!" he cursed. "More than thirty minutes had passed since Ferris had contacted me."

Chapter 33

It would be better if you let the woman and me go. I could make life in prison easier for you," Erik said.

Kalish laughed and the others grinned meanly. "Why should I? You belong to me. All by myself". He turned around and lifted something from the table. Erik could only recognize what it was when the dangerous guy turned again. In his hand, he held a toothpick. "In some countries," he said, "There are different ways to torture a person. With whips, chains and other percussion instruments. In the case of thieves in the Middle East, the hand is either chopped off or the skin is incinerated with a burning, glowing iron. Another way is to peel the skin off alive. Another variant would be to prick the eyes and burn them out. But I... I have something better for you. I will torture you in my way and enjoy it when you scream in pain".

Erik swallowed. What this devil had in mind for him was satanic. If he made only one sound of pain, then it was the beginning of the end. "I beg you. Don't do it," Erik pleaded with Satan.

"Ha. You are already whimpering? And before I even started? You disappoint me, bull!" Erik was silent. "Hmm ... Keeping silent? But not for long". The guy approached him. The ropes around the prisoner's joints were tightly tied. Kalish's left hand grabbed Erik's right hand. Only the thumb stood out. He held back the other fingers. With his right hand, Kalish held the toothpick between his thumb and forefinger.

Steadily, he led the small pointed piece of wood to Erik's right thumb. Then, he pushed it under his fingernail with full force. Blood splashed from this small, narrow wound and dripped to the floor. Erik saw stars flashing before his eyes. The pain was unbearable and salty tears came out of his eyes. Despite the sweat dripping from his forehead, he kept his mouth closed. 'It hurts as hell!' He thought and breathed quickly, heart racing.

"Do you like it, my friend? Oh, excuse me, I forgot. I am not your friend. Thus, I will continue".

Chapter 34

At some point, the cops reached Riverside and discovered Ferris's car. The detective saw the cars coming. He got out of his car and walked towards them. They stopped in front of him. But before that, the cops had turned off the blue lights and sirens. Ferris appeared next to the Captain's wagons. The captain got out.

"He's still in the warehouse. I was briefly there and tried to get in. But the iron door leading inside was closed and none of the motorcyclists showed up".

"That was careless," said the Captain. "It could have gone wrong".

"Sorry, but I wanted to scout the situation," Ferris apologized.

"It's all right". The captain turned around and spoke to the men.

"It appears that Detective Ferris has located the nest of these rats. But we have to be careful because they are armed. As a precaution, keep your weapons ready and shoot only in case of emergency. You," he pointed at three men, "secure the rear side of the hall. As for the others, come with me from the front. Let's go". The group, led by the captain, walked quietly towards the block of flats. They circumnavigated it and stood in front of the warehouse.

"I want to know what's going on inside," whispered Tom Stone. "Look through the windows". He meant those on the right and above the iron door. Two men moved to the wall while the others approached the metal door. One of the two men standing by the wall wanted to climb on the other's shoulders to see what was going on inside, but failed.

Chapter 35

Kalish grabbed one of those cursed toothpicks again and approached Erik again. "I wouldn't do it if I were you," Erik gasped in his sweat and the tears that had mixed. All of his clothes were wet from the sweat. The shirt was literally stuck to his body.

"And why not?"

"Because I... oh, you wouldn't understand".

This sadist said to Erik, "Speak".

Erik pronounced these sentences in a serious manner. "The night my father died and I arrested you, I took over my father's inheritance. A dangerous legacy. If you made me scream, it would mean your death. But you would not believe it and even the rest of this world, too. We would be doomed".

These words had impressed Kalish. Should he believe this possible madman or not?

"Erik", Helen Turner whispered to him from behind.

"Yes?" he said.

"Is what you are saying true?"

"It is the truth. But you have only experienced a small part of my secret". She remained silent afterwards.

That's what Kalish came back for. "Ha! I almost fell for your words. For that, I will punish you even harder".

"Don't do it."

"I do what I want to do".

"Then kill me. It would be better that way".

"No!" He grabbed Erik's index finger and rammed the toothpick under his nail. Erik bit his teeth together and pressed his lips together. The pain was unbearable, but he didn't scream.

"I want to hear you scream!" Kalish yelled at him. "Scream your pain out!". He enjoyed seeing this cop suffer as well as inflicting pain on him. "You don't want to? Then take more of this!" He already held another toothpick between his fingers. He pushed it into Erik's middle finger. This time, Erik could not bear any more of his pain because he was at the end of his strength. He screamed out his pain. The scream that Erik had given was so strong that the audience held their ears. This scream penetrated the smallest corner of the hall. The windows on the side walls exploded and broke. The fragments splashed around as dangerous projectiles.

In front of the warehouse, the captain called out to his people, "Take cover". The cops ducked instinctively as the rain of broken glass rained down on them. A moment later, it was over. The captain didn't care if they heard him in there or not. He only knew that he had to act quickly. "Break the door open. Quickly!". That was easier said than done because the door was made of iron. Despite the good tools they had with them, the policemen needed an eternity.

Meanwhile, there was dead silence inside the hall. Suddenly, everyone felt as the air changed. It somehow smelled different. But what people saw now was incredible. They doubted their minds. Erik's body began to glow. "I warned you. Now the beginning of the end has come," he said panting. The glow increased in intensity. The light formed into a round ball above his head. It was pure energy. Kalish retreated. The table was behind him. And behind it was Petit and the rest of the gang.

'You won't get me,' he thought. At that moment, he jumped to the right with a standing pike roll. There was the wooden door leading to the pier and was not closed. The moment he was pacing away, the energy ball dissolved and shot forward a flash of energy. Instead of hitting Kalish, it hit Petit and the others. The giant's colossus, like the others, was shaken like an electric shock. Then the man tilted forward and hit the table. It broke apart because of the weight and Petit fell to the ground dead with the splintered remains of wood. The same happened to the others. Like dead flies, they collapsed one by one and didn't stand up anymore. The only ones who survived were Conti and Travis. They've been sitting in the corner and didn't move. They did not know what to react. Helen Turner had survived, too, although the energy grazed her legs. The remaining energy returned to Erik and disappeared into his body.

Chapter 36

Stop! Hold it right there!" shouted a voice from the left. But Kalish didn't stick to that when he stormed out the door. He had barely escaped death and didn't think of getting caught like that. He continued zigzagging. "Stop or I'll shoot!" the voice shouted again. It was one of the three cops on the back of the warehouse who had called. He also fired a warning shot into the air. Kalish didn't care in the least. He kept running. Two more steps separate him from the East River. The water was black as night. He repelled himself and flew with a head jump towards the dark water. He heard shots while falling. The bullets were for him. These flew around his ears. A bullet hit him on his right leg. He screamed briefly before piercing the surface of the water and dove in. He didn't know what was happening above him. Kalish dived deeper and had only thought to save himself. Kalish also had another thought. He wanted to avenge himself more on the bull who had condemned him to go to safety. Full of hate, he swam away in the depth and was not seen anymore.

Chapter 37

The time was 24:50. The metal door gave way. With their weapons drawn out, the cops penetrated the warehouse. The captain followed. What they saw there made them swallow back several times. "What happened here?" whispered Tom Stone. No one knew the answer. The cops swarm out. They examined the men on the ground and could only determine their death. Conti and Travis also saw them. They sat tied up in a corner and lived. Two cops lifted them up and led them past the dead bodies of the motorcycle gang.

"Fenton!" the captain shouted and hurried towards the tied man. Erik sat in the chair and didn't move.

He whispered "Captain," when he heard his name was called. "What are you doing here?"

"I've come to get you out of a tight spot".

'You're late,' he thought. Tom Stone untied Erik Fenton. Then he went to the woman behind him and untied her as well. She stood up and hurried to Erik. He had already got up. Still, a little wobbly on his feet, but he stood. With the finger of his left hand, he had pulled the toothpicks out of his right. With each one, he felt pain in his fingers. These were bloody. The red juice ran out of them and dripped to the floor. His hand and arm trembled.

Helen was with Erik and threw herself at his neck. "I was so scared," she sobbed. Erik held her body with his left arm. He held the right one outside, so as not to pollute her with the blood.

"The Devil!" screamed someone at the iron door. "He has the Devil in him". It was Max Conti who screamed so loud when he was led away.

"It seems to me that the two of them will end up back at our station," said the Captain. But Erik Fenton and Helen Turner did not hear him. They were still standing close together.

"Sir?" said someone behind Tom Stone.

He turned around. "Yes?"

"These men here are dead. They're all dead. I don't understand," the cop said, reporting to the captain.

"I understand even less. But Mr. Fenton will answer a few questions".

"Sir?" someone else spoke now. It was one of the cops who came from the back of the warehouse.

"Somebody came out of the hall and escaped. He jumped into the East River and didn't show up again".

"That's Kalish," Erik told them who had been listening. He had taken a white handkerchief out of his jacket's pocket and wrapped it around his hand.

"Damn!" cursed Tom Stone. "We almost had him." The fact that this guy got away from him was worming him. Then, he asked Erik, "alright. But one thing I want to know is what this is." He pointed to the many corpses on the ground. "Who killed these men?"

"That is a long story. I will explain it later. I just want to get away from here. Do you mind?"

"Yes, of course. But don't you want to wait for the ambulance I ordered earlier? The wounds on your fingers don't look very good. You, Miss, also need medical help."

"Fine," said Erik. "We're waiting for the ambulance". The two of them walked to the wooden door leading to the pier. Erik walked to the pier and looked at the dark water. Then he raised his head, breathed in the air several times, which smelled of water, and looked at the night sky. Few stars shone brightly. "I have failed," he mumbled to himself. "I have failed".

Helen Turner stood behind him. "Erik," she whispered, "I still don't know what happened and what's bothering you, but we both will manage it together, okay?"

He said nothing. He turned away, took a few steps along the pier and Helen Turner followed.

Chapter 38

New Mexico. This was the center for research for the search for extraterrestrial life forms. In front of the building, there were countless parabolic mirrors, or the radio telescopes that capture signals from space. Jack Clark sat in one of the institute's soft armchairs. He was surrounded by expensive and complicated equipment. It was a quiet night. Nothing of any importance. Jack had put his legs on top of each other on the table. On his head, he wore headphones and listened to soft music. Suddenly, he was bitten by a snake. He tore it off his head and dropped it. He immediately took his legs off the table and jumped up from the chair.

"Ow!" he screamed in pain. His ears were still deaf from the noise he had heard. He used his finger to clear out his ears and breathed in and out quickly. He wanted to get rid of this deafness. Jack swallowed his saliva several times as if he were landing on a plane. Only now did he feel better. Then he thought about it. What a sight had that been! He had never experienced anything like it before. He couldn't think much about it, because something happened again. The devices started to work without having been touched. Instinctively, Jack pushed a button next to the table and the alarm in the institute went off. You could hear the siren in the corridors everywhere. After a few moments, some men stood in the control room, where Jack Clark sat on the armchair again.

"What's going on?!" shouted one of the men who had come in. It was the director of the institute.

"Look at that," Clark said, looking into the monitor. The man stood behind Clark and looked into the computer monitor.

"That's not possible," he whispered, "That's impossible". The other men also saw that but didn't say anything. It was clear to everyone in the room that these devices have gone crazy. Usually, the parabolic mirrors outside the station had to receive messages from outer space and play them into the devices. But here, it was their way around.

The devices took up an inaudible code and passed it on to the bowls. This signal was combined in the middle of one of the large parabolic mirrors. Then, it sent the signal out into space at incredible speed. The men, who stood in front of the monitor and were amazed, only saw a bright beam shooting into the vastness of the universe. It was swallowed by darkness and was not seen anymore. The devices began to work normally again.

"Wow!" one said. "What was that?"

"I have no idea," said the superior, "but maybe Mr. Clark can tell us something".

"Me? I don't know anything. I am clueless just like you. I've never seen anything like that before."

"But something must have caused this phenomenon. Please tell me what you did before it started".

"Nothing! I was sitting on this chair listening to music on my headphones. Then I ripped the headphones off my head because something loud came up. But I don't know what it was. But...wait. I think it sounded like a scream. Yes, exactly...like a scream".

Unbeknownst to these people, it was specifically at this time that Erik Fenton had screamed out his pain.

"Hmm," the boss made a sound and scratched his cheek.

"Do you think I'm crazy?" Clark asked him.

"After seeing it with my own eyes, I can't believe it. However, we must certainly pass this incident onto the authorities".

Chapter 39

Iceland. Kopasker Seismographic Institute. This institute is located outside the city. All underground activities of the famous geysers and volcanoes are analyzed and exploited here. A few seismographs were located in a large room. These registered the P, S and L waves; P for compression-W, S for shear-W, and L for love-W ground motion. One of these devices captured an impulse. The nib jerked back and forth and drew different waves on a sheet of paper. Michel Olsen, an employee of this institute, stood by this device and looked at the wave patterns. He mumbled, "Strange," to himself. He called his station manager to him, who stood on the other side of the room. "Sir, can you please come over here?". His superior agreed and came over after a few minutes.

"What is it?"

"Look at this pattern. This seems so familiar to me".

"Yes, I remember. You are right. We had that a few weeks ago". That was the moment when Erik took over his father's inheritance.

"But this one is not quite comparable with the first pattern".

"Right," said Olsen. "The first one was only a weak vibration. We couldn't find out where it came from until today. It's possible that it was only a striping. But this one is much stronger".

"That could give an earthquake of a Magnitude 4 ," said Olsen's superior.

"We'll find out soon enough." Olsen went to the other devices and checked the strength of the waves. He calculated the exact location of the earthquake through some measurements he found through the computer. He had the sheet printed out and presented it to his superior.

He continued to look at the pen and thought about it.

"Sir, look at that," Olsen said. He passed on the sheet of paper.

The director of the institute had never seen anything like it before. "You sure you didn't miscalculate?" he asked.

"I'm positive I didn't, Sir".

"But that's impossible. There are no fault gaps there. Normally, the eruptions are far below the ground. But these are... I don't understand".

"Me neither," said Olsen. Then they sounded the alarm. "The authorities won't very pleased and even the skippers on their ships who might be in this area". Olsen stepped up to the telephone and sounded the alarm.

Chapter 40

Greenland. The weather was cloudy that afternoon. The sun's rays couldn't penetrate through the thick clouds. The ship split the water in two. It was near Crown Prince Christian Land. That was on the western side of this country. The skipper of this ship was Ted Risk. He came from Spitsbergen and was on his way back to Canada with his friend and sailor Sam. Ted grumbled "Fucking weather," to himself.

"I agree," said Sam, who stood next to him at the helm and concentrated. He couldn't see very far because of this cloudy weather. The machines were running at only half power. After about ten minutes, the visibility became a little better.

"Well, would you look at that. Someone must have heard us," the skipper said. The pointed corner and the beginning of Crown Prince Land lay In front of them. It was a huge sight. Hundreds of meters of ice walls piled up in front of them. Whole walls of clear and glittering ice shining in the sunlight. "Do you smell the air?"

"Oh, I smell it," Sam said. The two of them enjoyed this moment, which immediately changed.

"Do you feel that?" Sam asked.

"Yes, as if the ground is vibrating under my feet".

"Exactly, but are our machines causing it?" They looked at the water. It was quiet earlier. But they saw that the water was throwing light waves. Ted Risk turned off the ship's engines with a flick of the wrist.

"It is the water that's vibrating. I've never seen ocean water vibrate like this before," the skipper said.

"This could be a sea quake," said Sam, who held the steering wheel tight.

"How do you know?"

"I experienced it once on my trip to the East. I'll tell you that wasn't a piece of cake".
The skipper, who was a tough guy, swallowed his saliva. He asked, "Do you think so?"

"And if I did?". The vibration grew stronger. The ship danced on the water like a nut bowl. A bit further ahead, the water bubbled so strong that countless fish shot out of the water, turned in the height, and fell back clapping.

"It's an earthquake!" Sam shouted to the skipper. "Hold on tight".
Ted Risk held on to the side door and looked forward. "There!" he shouted and pointed his finger at it. In front of them were the high ice towers. They saw a wall coming down and sinking into the sea. Behind this wall, a rock came to light. Nobody would have guessed that something like this was hiding behind the ice walls. But that was not all. The rock consisted of a half arch. The interior and lower part consisted again of ice and snow.

"Looks like a frozen grotto or cave," Sam said in the boat swing. He and Ted watched the spectacle, warily. The rock trembled. The ice gave way at the inner edges. It crunched and detached itself from the rock. An iceberg detached itself from the indentation of this rock. This slowly drifted towards the ship.

"Damn!" shouted the skipper. "He's going to ram us." Despite the strong waves, he started the ship's engines.

Sam tore the rudder to the starboard to escape the huge iceberg. They succeeded. Both of them puffed deeply when they had dodged the mountain. After a while, as quick as the quake had begun, as abruptly as it had stopped. What remained was an indentation in the rock, which would be covered in snow and ice again sometime. Yet, that was not the end. "There's something wrong," Sam said.

"You're right," gave Ted Risk back. "Look at that". What they saw was incredible. This iceberg questioned all the laws of nature. The skipper reached for the radio and made an emergency call. This was heard by the Coast Guard of Spitsbergen. It roared in the line. A male voice came forward.

"This is Coast Guard Spitsbergen. Over."

"Here is the Fishleg. Captain Ted Risk on the radio".

"Hello, captain," said the man. He knew the captain of the ship. "It's me, Björn. What's up?"

"Hello, Björn. We got into an earthquake, a sea quake. Maybe it wasn't an earthquake. We aren't sure. In any case, the water vibrated wildly".

"It was a sea quake. We just got this message from Iceland. Did it harm you?"

"No, not that, but it did something unusual."

"What is it?" did Björn want to know from the Coast Guard.

"A mountain of ice has detached itself from a wall and has come down. Behind the ice wall, there was a rock. In it, there was an iceberg that had come loose. It almost rammed us. But we got away. However, the iceberg is drifting against the current".

"Are you kidding me? There's no such thing!"

"I'm telling you; it should be drifting North and not South. That iceberg is not normal. There is something wrong".

"All right. I will follow the matter. But if you want to fool me, then you have to pay the next round at the regulars' table, when you are again on your way here".

"Alright," said Ted Risk and said goodbye. Then, he continued his trip to Canada.

Chapter 41

Björn walked from the radio to the computer. With fast fingers, he typed on the keyboard. This coastguard station was especially equipped and had a weather satellite in space. It was primarily used to determine whether bad or good weather forecasts were coming from the North. Subsequently, the environment of the sea would be taken under the magnifying glass. Finally, a specialist has to take immediate measures if ships were in distress. Ships were often rammed by ice floes.

Björn looked into the monitor. At first, some data appeared. Nothing unusual was displayed. He turned his head to the right. There stood the monitor of the radar screen. The pictures from the satellite appeared. "Ted Risk," he murmured to himself, "If you've drunk too much, you will already see ghosts". He took a good look at everything. He discovered some ice floes drifting down from the East coast. The drift ice was not a great danger for shipping. The thaw quickly opened. But what was that? He looked more closely and discovered something else. There was a dot on the screen that was not supposed to be there. 'This Ted Risk was right. There's an iceberg but it's not just a small one,' he thought. And the incredible thing was that it was drifting against the current. "What is happening now?" he said to himself. The dot on the monitor suddenly seemed transparent. Björn knocked against the monitor of the screen. "That's not possible!" he exclaimed. The dot disappeared. What remained were only the few ice floes he had seen before. He immediately sounded the alarm. He radioed all the ships and informed the Icelandic authorities that an iceberg was coming towards them.

Chapter 42

The message was recorded by the local authorities. They sent a ship along the coast of Greenland. The captain of the ship wants to see for himself what was going on. The person who had informed them could not give any details. He had only spoken of an iceberg drifting against the current, which has now disappeared. After almost two days on sea, the captain saw the iceberg. It drifted right towards them. The strange thing was that a light fog had formed around the iceberg. That could be the answer why the radar couldn't locate it. The fog made it looked like it disappeared. The captain passed the message on and then tried to get the ship near the iceberg. When he was close enough, something strange happened. The ship's controls, engines and technical equipment failed, as if someone had pulled the power plug out of them. Every necessary measure was done to make the ship gain power again, but their attempts failed. Only when they were driven away by the current and separated a few meters from the iceberg did the machines start to run again. The captain felt as if the iceberg didn't want anyone near it. That's why he remained at a distance and just followed it.

Two days later, the iceberg drifted through the Danemarkstrasse, which was located between Iceland and Greenland. For the inhabitants of Iceland, this was an unusual phenomenon. The newspapers had already reported it. They drove to the coasts to look at the iceberg and took pictures.

The driving mountain was accompanied on its way by the Cost Guards of Greenland and Iceland. This was due to safety and to prevent any unprecedented casualties.

The iceberg drifted further towards Cape Farvel. Cape Farvel was the Southernmost point of Greenland. It takes almost a day and a half to get there. Shortly, it drove through the Labrador Basin to Newfoundland and from there, along the whole coast of Canada.

The Canadian authorities, respectively the Coast Guards, took over the escort of the iceberg. The Icelandic ships turned around and returned to their territorial water. It was not long before the American Coast Guards replaced the role of the Canadian ships. The iceberg continued to drift along the American coast. The media had long since captured this phenomenon. The news and newspapers reported about the iceberg. The Coast Guards were seconded and the Navy was called in. They had to find out why the iceberg was drifting in their direction. A small cruiser, as well as some ships of the navy, accompanied the strange iceberg on its way. At one point, one of the men serving on the cruiser reported something new about this mysterious case. "Sir!" shouted the man sitting in front of the radar.

The commander of the ship came over. "You called?"

"Yes, Sir. I have some values here that you should take a look at".

The supervisor looked at the monitor. "Unbelievable. The iceberg is slowing down and also the fog around the lump, is clearing".

The radar screen had been able to locate the iceberg again and showed it again on the monitor. "It seems to me that it would like to end its journey here."

The cruiser was near Nantucket Island. An island off Rhode Island. "Okay. Let's try to capture it". In no time, there was a hectic rush on the ship. With a cannon from the stern, one had shot a harpoon like the whale catchers do, in the direction of the iceberg. The upper part of the harpoon drilled deep into the ice. "We have it!" called the man who had shot down the harpoon. "Pull the rope tight!" he gave the order to another man. He stood behind him and activated the winch. The rope tightened.

The commander of the ship shouted "Good work, men!" down to his crew. Then he turned around and approached an officer. "Hard to port and slowly ahead. We'll pull the lump of ice to New York".

"Yes, Sir". The officer did as he was told.

One day later, the cruiser was in New York Harbor. It took them so long, because the iceberg was heavier to pull than they thought. The ship now turned its course and headed for Fort Tilden with just a few knots. Some helicopters of the well-known television stations circled around the ship. They sent these fascinating footages live to every household. It was already a huge spectacle. When the ship came near Fort Tilden, the helicopters had to turn back because it was a restricted area. But the media continued to broadcast and wrote their stories on the local papers. The newspaper makers rubbed their hands because their circulation shot up from writing. The commander of the ship did not care what was being written or broadcast. For him, it was important to bring this iceberg to its destination and it was within reach. Fort Tilden was the only base in New York with a large hall that led into the sea. Here in this hall, ships were baptized and later launched. Today, it was the other way around. At some point, the iceberg was released from the ship and pulled into the hall with powerful winches. The head of the operations, a sergeant of the military, called out to the man behind him. "Go! Let's go. Another good ten meters, then we'll have it in." The man who operated the machines nodded. He knew what to do.

After a few moments, it was time. The man stopped the machines. The iceberg landed safe in the warehouse. The entrance of this hall was closed on the sea-side. The heavy metal doors moved towards each other from the sides, until they collided with each other. A muffled noise filled this hall. "Drain the water slowly but surely. Who knows if it will tip over?"

Since the iceberg was in a water lock, it was easy to drain the seawater. Almost half an hour passed until it was gone. "Okay," called the sergeant. "Down with the ropes". Some men pulled the metal ropes. When these were down, a man in a white smock was peeling himself out of the gawking military crowd. He had a narrow face. He also wore glasses and had brown hair.

"Well, Professor?" meant a voice next to him. It belonged to the professor's assistant.

"What? Impressive. I've never seen an iceberg this close before. I will certainly not get bored when I examine it". The professor pronounced these words as if he were examining a human being.

"What are you still standing around for?!" a man shouted. It was the sergeant. The gawking soldiers heard his voice and there was movement in these men. They disappeared from the iceberg and did their real work.

In the back corner of the hall after the iceberg, stood a wooden hut that served as an office. The soldiers brought countless technical devices into the room and placed them on the table. There were computers, measuring instruments and many other things that the professor needed for his work. "Yes, put them up like that," he gave the instructions.

The assistant connected the plugs of the devices and after a few minutes, he switched them on. "It will take a little longer," he said, "until we can use them".

"It's all right," the professor said. He's been working with his assistant Jeff Dick for six months already. He found that this young man could one day become his successor if he continued so intensively.

In the meantime, the sergeant walked through the hall and stopped in front of a metal door that opened. Daylight penetrated into the artificially lit hall. On the threshold, a man with countless awards on his uniform stands. "Sir," the sergeant stood in front of the man and greeted him in a military manner.

He returned the greeting. "Sergeant. Lead me to the one who is examining the iceberg," he spoke with a cold voice.

"Yes, Sir. This way, Sir". Since there were many cables on the ground, the man walked behind the sergeant. Every soldier who met the two greeted the highest-ranking officer. They came closer to the wooden hut.

"Who's responsible for solving the riddle?" asked the man.

"It was—" said the sergeant as both entered the room of the hut. He was interrupted by the professor who had recognized the voice behind him, and turned around.

"It's me, General Cobe." Surprised, the general stopped in front of the professor.

"You?"

"Yes, it's me."

"Prof. Dr. Stanley Poken".

"I hear that you have correctly formulated my title and my name, General Cobe".

"What the hell is he doing on this military base?" the general addressed the sergeant.

"He was allowed to, Sir. He got a letter from the president himself. He will examine the iceberg".
The general didn't like the fact that this professor was here. He gritted his teeth, turned around and walked away. The sergeant looked at the professor, shrugged his shoulders and ran after the general.

"I'll see you again soon," the professor spoke quietly to himself.

The assistant next to him asked, "You know him?"

"Yes, I did. It's been about five years since I had the pleasure of meeting him," He answered, emphasizing the word pleasure in a sarcastic way.

"May I ask what happened?"

"It is better if you don't know". The professor turned back to his equipment, which was now ready to go.

In the hall, the sergeant stood next to the general and listened to what he commanded him. "This professor..." he murmured.

"Yes, Sir. What about him?"

"I want you to watch him closely. Everything he does and everything he finds out. Everything, but also really just everything I want to know. You shall give me a report every hour. Have I made myself clear?"

"Yes, Sir," the sergeant spoke and greeted the general. He returned the greeting.

"Resign, Sergeant". Then, the two separated.

While the general moved to the door outside, the sergeant walked through the hall. He gave some instructions to his men. "So," said Prof. Dr. Poken "Let's go to work. Is the device ready yet?" he asked Jeff Dicks.

"Yes," he gave him the confirmation.

"Then, go". Both of them came out of the hut and approached the iceberg. The young man had a Geiger counter in his hand. He had already switched it on when he approached the white mass and swiveled the Geiger counter from right to left.

"Hmm... Normal beat," he said as he looked at it. "Nothing unusual".

"Then, we'll take a sample," the professor said. He scraped something off the iceberg. Then he brought the ice onto the laboratory table that had been set up earlier. Under the microscope, the frozen snow looked normal. The microscope showed nothing. The professor entered the ice into the computer via the microscope. It took a while until the data appeared on the monitor. "There. Now we're getting something," he said and was astonished at the same time.

The data indicated the age of the ice. 9th century was written on the monitor. "An old ice. Practically, it has not been changed since that time. Some rock particles on the iceberg crust have been analyzed. See?" the professor stated and pointed with the finger on the data. The assistant just nodded. "There must be an explanation onto why the iceberg disabled the ship's system controls".

"It was the fog around that mountain that did that," said Jeff Dicks.

"Yes, but how did it come into Being? There must be something there".

"We must have missed something," said the assistant.

"But what?" murmured Prof. Dr. Poken. Both of them were at loss until the young man had an idea.

"We have the drill with us under our equipment. Maybe the secret is inside the iceberg".

"That's it," said the professor and snapped his finger and praised him. "Let's drill a hole in the ice to see what's inside."

A quarter of an hour later, everything was ready. The two scientists approached the iceberg with a special drilling machine and a matching drill of two meters in length. Since the drill was too heavy to carry, it stood on a mobile base. Two soldiers, equipped with thick gloves, held the front part of the drill in their hands. Jeff Dicks pressed the start button and the drill turned slowly. He penetrated the ice and ate his way through. The two soldiers now took their hands away as the drill found its way by itself. It came through by a meter. Then the ice began to get thicker and harder.

"It will be hard to penetrate further," said Jeff Dicks.

"Keep going but slower, please," said the professor.

The assistant kept pressing against the drill, until he noticed that it did not go on. "Something seems to stop the drill. I can't get any further".

"Then pull it out".

"How deep was it in?" asked the assistant.

"Over a meter and a half". The young man was pulling on the mobile vehicle. He moved backwards and let the drill slowly turn in the other direction. Subsequently, he got the drill out better. The two soldiers stood again in front and stopped the drill. Jeff Dicks was now standing with the two soldiers. At every turn of the drill, one could see the different ice layers of the iceberg. Once white, then again dark and finally a bit bright. He looked at the layers until he discovered something on the tip of the drill. "Professor," he spoke excitedly "Look at this".

"What is it?"

"The tip. It is not covered with ice. It looks as if the drill has drilled its way into wood".

The professor looked at it. "You are right. They are wood chips. I want to examine them". The professor took the wood chips from the drill and brought them to the microscope in his hollow hand. He placed them on a small glass plate and pushed them under the delicate apparatus. He showed him the chips down to the last detail.

"Let's see if the computer can tell us anything more about it". He brought the small glass pane to the computer. Using ultra-modern laser technology, the computer scanned the wood chips. Less than a quarter of an hour passed and the computer had the data.

"What?" said the professor. "That's very interesting. Like the ice we analyzed, these wood chips are almost the same age".

"From the 9th century?" Surprised, the assistant said this date.

"Yes. Maybe a few years earlier".

"Then the only possible solution for this mystery is in the iceberg".

"Yes".

"Sergeant," the professor called the man to himself.

"Yes, professor?" said the sergeant, who walked up to him and stopped next to him.

"We must melt the iceberg. Do you have something like a furnace?"

"Furnace? No, the military doesn't have such a thing, but I could find you some powerful heat lamps. If placed correctly, in some places," he pointed from left to right, in the middle and down from above, "We could melt the ice and quicker".

"How fast?" asked the professor.

"On such frozen dimensions, about a week. Maybe even earlier".

"Good. Then please get me those radiators". The sergeant walked to the telephone. He got the phone number from his shirt breast pocket. It was General Cobe's number he had received earlier. He typed it in and immediately heard the General's icy voice on the other side.

"Yes?" he said of himself.

"General Cobe, Sir. This is Sergeant Rock".

"Speak".

"Something interesting seems to be about to happen, Sir."

"Don't beat about the bush, Sergeant. Go to the point".

"Yes, Sir. Prof. Dr. Poken has discovered something. He doesn't know exactly what it could be, but he tried to penetrate the iceberg via a drill, until the tip of the drill couldn't get any further. There seems to be a wood or something hard. In any case, wood chips have accumulated at the drill tip. The analysis of the chips has shown that they could originate from the 9th century".

General Cobe said in astonishment, "There's something else in there, I suppose?"
"The professor agrees. He wants to melt the iceberg, and he asked me to do it. We need here about four or five heat emitters, Sir".

The general was thinking. "Good. I'll have them brought to you. If anything happens when the ice starts to melt, give me a call".

"Yes, Sir," Sergeant Rock spoke into the receiver and hung up. Half an hour later, the radiant heaters were delivered to Fort Tilden by helicopter and brought into the hall. The sergeant called out to the soldiers, "Put them up there and there". Nine of the heavy radiators were placed around the iceberg and switched on. The heat that united in the hall was very pleasant as the iceberg emitted icy cold breeze.

"Now the wait begins," said the professor.

"You're right," said Jeff Dicks.

"It is already evening. Nothing will happen until tomorrow. Let's go home," the professor said.

Chapter 43

The next day. Ten o'clock in the morning. The rooms of Prof. Dr. Poken and Jeff Dicks were adjacent to each other. They were on the premises of Fort Tilden. They only had to walk for ten minutes until they reached the hall. When the two pushed open the metal door and entered, they stopped in amazement. Suddenly, something happened. Jeff Dicks swallowed and the professor was overwhelmed. Sergeant Rock approached both of them. "Do you know what that could be?" he asked.

"Oh, yes," he replied.

"That's good," he said, "Because I already told General Cobe. He will arrive here in a few minutes". The professor didn't care what the man before him said. His eyes were still glued on the iceberg. The heat emitters had melted the front and the upper part of the ice. Something was brought out that seemed almost impossible. Now the professor knew. Inside the iceberg there was a hidden ship, which was slowly freed from the ice. But it wasn't a simple ship. It was a ship from the past.

"What the hell is that?!" shouted a voice behind the professor. It was the icy voice of the general. The two scientists stood in front of the iceberg and turned around. The general walked towards the two and stopped next to them. "So? What is that? What do you already know about that thing?"

"Nothing real significant yet. We've just arrived, but I know something for sure," the professor said.

"And what do you know?"

"That this is a Dragon."
"A what?"

"A Dragon. That's what the ancient warriors from the North called their ships". General Cobe did not understand what the professor meant. "Tell me something. Haven't you gone to school?" the scientist asked the general.

"Of course, I did".

"It seems to me that you have learned nothing from World History class".

"How dare you accuse me of such a thing!" the General raised his harsh voice.

"Do you always rain your temper on, General? If you'd paid attention at school, you'd know".

General Cobe stopped talking, and swallowed his saliva that had accumulated in his mouth. He breathed heavily before saying anything again. "If you think I haven't learned anything from it, you can definitely enlighten me".

"It's nice of you to ask me, but I don't know everything".

"Aha!" said the general.

"But an old friend of mine can tell you much more about it. Would it be pleasant for you if I called him and ordered him here?"

The general gritted his teeth. It did not suit him that another uninvolved person would appear here. But what was left for him. He wanted to solve the riddle. "Fine. Call him. In the meantime, remove Sergeant's heat radiator from over there".

"Yes, Sir". The sergeant waved to some soldiers, who immediately carried out the work. The professor walked to his laboratory and pulled out a telephone book from his briefcase. The telephone was hanging next to the door on the wall. He typed in the Washington D.C. phone number and heard the dial tone. Then, someone picked up on the other end.

"Hello?" someone was speaking. It was a female voice.

"Hello, Sheila. It's me. Stanley".

"Stanley! What a surprise. How have you been all these years?"

"Good. And you?"

"Likewise. Thank you".

"How are the children?"

"They're out there somewhere looking at girls."

The professor had to laugh. "That's supposed to be like that, isn't it?"

Sheila made her comment, "Right. You and Frank were no different when you were Sixteen".

"How right you are".

"Are you looking for Frank?" she asked.

"That's one of the reasons I'm calling. I have discovered something that will knock him out".

"Does it have something to do with his work?"

"Oh, yes. It's about—no, he should come here himself. Then, he will see it. Do you know where he is?"

"Yes. He is in New York at a lecture".

"I see. Do you have his phone number?"

"Yes. Just a moment, please". The professor heard it rustling at the other end.

'Sheila is looking for the phone number in the agenda again. It will surely be scribbled on some piece of paper again,' he thought. He knew her well and the 'order' in her agenda.

"Yes. I have them". The woman gave it to him, and he said goodbye to her. And he proceeded to call Frank. Two hours later, a car appeared in front of Fort Tilden. The car was stopped for inspection and a man, in his mid-Forties with dark hair, looked out of the car.

"My name is Frank Waldon. General Cobe and Prof. Dr. Stanley Poken are expecting me".

The soldier at the entrance nodded as he looked on his list. "You are expected. Turn right at the crossroads and go straight on to the hangar". Then the soldier gave the signal to lift the barrier. The barrier went up and cleared the way. The car drove on and reached the hall after a few minutes. Frank Waldon got out of the car and saw someone coming towards him. "Sir," spoke a sergeant. "I am Sergeant Rock. You are Mr. Waldon?".

"Yes, I am".

"Please follow me".

The two men walked to the hall. Before they entered, a metal door opened and a general and another man stepped outside. "Stanley!" called Frank.

"Hello, Frank. Good to see you. Thank you for coming so quickly".

"You were lucky. The lecture was just over".

"May I introduce General Cobe to you?". The two of them shook hands.

"So. What's so important that you called me here?"

"It has something to do with your work. That's all I could tell you on the phone".

"But General Cobe can tell me, for sure".

"Yes. It's top secret. You understand?" Frank nodded.

"What do you know about dragon ships?"

"Is that what they call secret?" Frank Walden asked a little irritated.

"Just answer me this question. Or rather, tell me in detail what you know about it historically".

Frank cleared his throat. "Well. We know that America is from C.C...".

"C.C.?" asked the general.

"Yes. Cristoforo Colombo, an Italian, under the Spanish flag. But he was not the first. In the 7th-9th century it was the Nordic peoples of Scandinavia. More precisely, it was the Vikings who landed here on this continent. Archaeological excavations revealed that they were the first. The Vikings were skilled boat builders. Without a compass, which did not exist that time, they oriented themselves on their seafaring trips according to the stars and the sun. On their raids along the coasts, they sowed death. Violence and brutality surpassed everything known in history. These horrors of the North Seas worshiped a pagan war god named Thor. For every Viking, it was the most sacred wish to die with a sword in his hand so that he could be taken into Walhall".

"What is Walhall?" asked the general.

"This is the whereabouts of the Vikings who died in battle according to their beliefs".

"What's the next step?"

"It would take too long to go into the smallest detail. Anyway, there were other gods. For example, the goddess Hel. For the imagination or belief of every Viking at that time, the earth was a flat disk. If you went off course, you would fall over the edge of the world and fall into the realm of the goddess".

He took a short break and said, "May I ask you a question?"

"Yes, please."

"Have you ever read the English prayer book from that time?" Frank asked the General.

"No! How could I?"

"It says: Protect us, O Lord, from the wrath of the North men".

The General swallowed.

"You'll be amazed," the professor addressed the general. The sergeant also lost his spit when he heard this.

"Frank asked his friend, "Was that all?" Prof. Dr. Stanley Poken looked at the general. He nodded. The professor approached his friend.

"You once told me that you found something interesting during your research".

"Yes. An old script in the books of a Nordic couple. I was able to decipher it with a computer translation".

"What did it say?" asked General Cobe.

"Well, that a Viking ship disappeared in the 9th century. Just like that. But before that some initiates want to have seen something".

"What then?" The general was curious.

"Something unusual. It was a light. Something was shining, or completely enveloping the ship. Then it disappeared. So... General. They ask me some things. Why?"

"Just so".

"I don't believe you. I'm not just here to tell you a story. So! What is going on here".

"Did you hear about the iceberg that drifted so far?" asked the professor.

"Yes, of course. What about that?"

"Come in with us". The four men entered the hall. When Frank Walden saw the iceberg, he was overwhelmed. His heart was beating up to his neck when he saw the part of a ship looking out.

"A Drakkar," he whispered.

"A drunkar—what?" General Cobe spoke next to him.

"A Viking warship and maybe even the ship that disappeared. My God. The scripture had not lied". He walked with hesitant steps towards the bow, stopped in front of it and shook his head. He hadn't expected that. A dragon's head looked out of the iceberg.

"Impressive, isn't it?". The professor had pronounced these words.

"I am... I am speechless".

"That was me, too".

"Do you think the rest of the ship is still in iceberg?"

"I believe and suspect it already".

"Fantastic. I can hardly believe it".

The general interrupted the two and turned to Frank Walden. "How long can such a boat be?".

"About the length of this iceberg or what remains of it".

The general now asked the professor, "You don't have an exact data?"

"Yes, we do. When the iceberg was pulled in, I scanned it". He asked his assistant for the computer phrases. He brought them to them and politely introduced himself to Frank Waldon.

"Here," spoke the professor, who looked at the data. "60×30 meters. The height is 18 meters high".

"The draft," asked Frank Walden.

"Strange that you should ask me that. I should have realized earlier that it had almost no depth because normally icebergs are two thirds of the ice mass in the water. Only one third is at the top, but here it was exactly two meters fifty-two under the water surface. A miracle that we were able to push this iceberg into the hall".

"What else can you tell me about it?" said General Cobe.

"The most important thing you heard earlier" Frank Walden said.

"But yes. You mentioned something else about a light".

"I was able to read that from the old script. I can't tell you what it is all about. Prof. Dr. Poken is the expert for extraordinary phenomena".

"I know that too. But he can't tell me anything about it yet".

"Maybe later," the professor said.

"But I'm sure you can tell me what it is." The military man pointed his finger up to the bow.

"What do you mean?".

"Well, that. Those round things there. There, in the wood. Below the dragon's head. What could that be?".

The professor and Frank Walden stepped closer to the bow. "I need a ladder," said Frank. It was brought to him and he climbed it. His gaze remained stuck to the round things. "Those are... aren't they?".

"What?" the general shouted up from below.

"They are faces. Male faces and all wear a beard".

The professor spoke, "That's strange. Can you see how many there are?"

"I can count them already, but the ice must melt even more. Because I suppose, no, I think that under this one the row has to go on".

He was right, because only the front part was still to be seen. "I believe that this must be the first head of the sequence". He pointed at him. "It looks as if these faces are related to each other. The similarity is amazing".

"What do you say?" asked the professor. He had almost not understood him because he had spoken quietly.

"I said that these faces could be related. It's like a line of ancient men with their descendants".

"It is unbelievable. How do these faces get into the wood if the ship has always been in the iceberg?". The professor had asked this question and the question remained among those present.

'Yes, my friend,' Frank Waldon thought. 'How do these faces get into the wood'.

"Should we knock out the ice to see how far the heads go?" asked the general.

"Are you crazy?" said the man on the ladder. "One false blow and the ship would be destroyed for a part. The ship has an immeasurable value".

"It's all right," said the general. "It was only a suggestion".

'Yeah, a bad suggestion,' Frank Waldon thought. He knew that the others thought the same.

"What's the next step?" General Cobe said to the professor.

"We let nature run its course and continue as before".

"Good". Then he turned to Frank Waldon. "Please come down". The man did what the man told him.

When he stood next to him, he asked, "Can I stay here and support the professor in his work?

The general thought about it.

"What about your work? Don't you have to leave again?"

"Oh, that can wait. For me, only this count at the moment. So! How did you decide?"

"Good. But I want to be informed exactly what they find out".

"I will".

Chapter 44

Two days later. The dragon ship was almost free of ice. It was supported by wooden posts on the sides so it would not tip over. The posts were wet as the melting ice flowed down. The general stood with the sergeant in front of the ship. The other three men also stood there.

"And?" asked General Cobe. "What did it look like? What did you find out?"

Frank Waldon was the first to speak. "This is an unusual ship".

"What do you mean?"

"Look. Normal dragon boats are equipped with benches in the middle. Ancient vikings would take a seat and let the oars into the water. But this ship has a new, completely different construction. I don't want to say that the oars are missing. They are in the right position. One on top of the other, inside the shape of the ship. What I meant to say is that there is a kind of wooden roof above the rudder benches. Everything is covered. I don't know why, but I'll figure it out".

"You haven't examined it yet?"

"No, I wanted to wait until everything was dry. Because as soon as I put my foot on the planks, it can have consequences for the wood".

"The wood?"

"Yes. The water has attacked the wood so badly that I might leave my shoe prints behind. But tomorrow, when the ship may be dry, I will take the first step on it".

"Good," said the general. Then he asked the professor. "What did you find out?"

"Nothing yet. I still don't know why the fog around the iceberg has switched off the system controls of the ships. So far it is still a mystery, but I will solve it".

"What about the faces on the wood?"

"Based on our current findings, it could really be a line of ancestors. There are exactly 26 faces. Starting from the bow and extending to the stern. They're nicely and systematically distributed. The distance from one to the other is the same. But something is strange. The first face seems to be from the 9th century, visually. We found that out so far".

"What?" shouted General Cobe. "That is impossible. There can be no such thing. Are you sure?"

"We don't have time for jokes, General," said Frank Waldon. "We captured the individual faces with a reading laser, chased them through the computer and noticed something".

"Tell me."

"The last two faces, or rather, the last face could be from our time".

General Cobe was speechless. He lacked the words. That was unbelieveable. 'From our time, he say,' he thought. "But how is that possible?"

"We don't know, either. Unfortunately, we're still clueless," said the professor.

"Could the computer be wrong?"

"Only a human being can make mistakes on science. But the computer with systematically calculated data? I'm afraid not,"

"How old could the recent face be?" asked the general.

"Approximately, a few months," Frank Walden spoke. "The computer indicated around the month of May. Now we are at the end of August".

"The last face?"

"The only one without a beard is not older than three weeks".

"How is that possible?". The General was not the only one who wondered about all this. He thought until something occurred to him. "Can we pursue the matter in a different way?"

"What do you mean, General?" asked Frank Waldon.

"Well, you've analyzed the faces. The last two were from our time. Since we live in the age of computers, this should not be an obstacle. Let's chase these two through the face files of the main computer".

"It's a good idea," said the professor. "But what computer do you mean?"

"The Pentagon, FBI and CIA. We'll find out for sure".

"Very good. I'll give you a disk with the two faces on it," the professor said, walking to his lab.

After a few minutes, he was back with the general and gave it to him.

"Good luck with that" he said.

Then the general and the sergeant said goodbye to the two men and left the hall

Chapter 45

The computer center at Fort Tilden was as hectic as never before. The general was scaring up the computer people in charge. "You've got a two-million-dollar computer here. I want answers to both faces. Get to work," he said in a cold tone. Three people entered the data for the faces and let them go through. After a few minutes, they had the first one.

"Sir," spoke the one computer expert. "I got something here". The general looked over the man's shoulder. Then he moved to the right to look better at the monitor.

"That could be the one," the man said, "But he's dead. He was buried last May. His name was Erik Gunnarsson".

"Next," asked the general.

"Just a moment," the man spoke and typed with fast fingers into the keys. Some data appeared on the screen. It says:

Year of birth: 1929
Place of Residence: Unknown
Occupation: None
Family members: None
Remark: Registered in homeless shelters

"A tramp?" said the general. Then, he was called by another computer staff.

"Sir?". He turned to the right. "The computer located the other man".

"Who is it?". He bent forward to stare at the screen. A picture had appeared.

"It's a cop who'd left work. Thus, a former cop. He left the police service, one day after the death of the homeless". He had taken the data from the other computer over to himself. That's why he knew.

"Interesting," said the general.

"Yes, but that's not all. The man's name is Erik Fenton. Exactly the same first name as the bum".

"That is our man. Print everything we know about this man".

"Yes, Sir". The computer expert did as he was ordered. After a few moments, General Cobe had the data he needed. There was also a picture of Fenton. Then he called Sergeant Rock to him that afternoon.

"Here". He gave him the photo of Erik Fenton. "This is our man. Find out where he is right now".

"Do you have the address, Sir?"

"No. The form says he's moved out. But I know the best place to ask is the 70th police station in Brooklyn. This former cop worked under a Captain Tom Stone. Maybe this man knows where Mr. Fenton is".

The sergeant greeted the general. "I'll do my best, Sir". Minutes later, Sergeant Rock and a soldier of the base were on the way with a military jeep.

Chapter 46

The 70th Police Station. A knock came on the Captain's door. He sat on his comfortable chair and read the police reports. "Yes?" he shouted without looking. The office door opened.

"Sir," spoke one of the employees. "A Sergeant Rock from Fort Tilden is here. He wants to talk to you".

"Tell him to come inside".

The sergeant entered Tom Stone's office a few moments later. He spoke, "Hello," and shook hands with the captain.

"Sergeant Rock. Please take a seat". The captain offered the man a chair, but it stopped.

"A military sergeant is extremely rare for me to see. To what do I owe this visit to?"

"A visit is a must. I believe you have the information that I need".

"Shoot it off, Sergeant".

He took the photo out of the breast pocket and gave it to the captain. "I'm looking for this man. Can you help me find him?"

"Fenton," said the captain.

"That's the name. I'm looking for the man who knows his whereabouts".

"Why are you looking for him?"

"It's a military secret. You understand?"

The Captain didn't think and didn't say a word. 'What does this man want from Fenton?' he thought.

"Can you tell me where he is now?"

"Yes, I can, but I want you to tell me why you're looking for him first".

"The military needs him. It's about something extraordinary. That's all I can tell you".

"Extraordinary. Hmm... like that. Does this extraordinary thing have anything to do with a light?"

The sergeant became attentive. What did this captain know about a light? Frank Waldon was the only one who had reported on the word 'light'.

"That's exactly what I want to know about. What do you know about it, or can this Erik Fenton tell me more about it?"

"I don't know anything about it. It appeared briefly a few months ago and disappeared".

"Do you have a report about it?" the sergeant asked.

"Yes, I did".

"Can I have it?". The man just looked at the cop. "Don't get me wrong, but I really need your help".

"All right. I'll give you the report, but it's just a copy".

"That's enough for me".

The captain went to a filing cabinet. In a drawer he pulled out a report. "Here is my copy," and gave it to him.

"Thank you. But I still don't know where Mr. Fenton is".

"He is not here. He is with a friend in Saranac Lake. He is fishing there".

"Thank you, Captain. You have something good with me". The sergeant shook his hand and left the police building. Once outside, he got into the jeep and drove back to Fort Tilden.

Chapter 47

Back at Fort Tilden. The general was reading the report about Fenton. "I knew this Fenton was our man," General Cobe said and commented, "Interesting".

"Indeed, Sir. With all due respect, Sir, I'd like to bring the man in."

"Good suggestion, Sergeant Rock. Good work so far". General Cobe was known in military circles as a hard man. There was hardly ever any praise from him. But today, he produced it. For the sergeant, this was an honor.

"Thank you, Sir," he spoke with pride.

"So far so good. Bring the man here. You know where to find him".

"Sir, it's almost 6PM. It will be night and it will be difficult to find him. My suggestion would be if I started in the early morning hours with the helicopter. I'm sure he won't run away from Saranac Lake tonight".

The general was thinking. "Alright. Tomorrow at 5AM, you'll start. Take two more soldiers with you. You never know".

"Yes, Sir!" The sergeant saluted and disappeared from the general's field of vision.

'Fenton, huh,' he thought. 'You'll have to explain to me why your face is on the ship'.

Chapter 48

Fort Tilden. The time was 10PM. In the hall, where the dragon ship stood, it was still. Only the eight legs of the four soldiers could be heard as they walked through the hall. They were guarding the ship.

"Nothing's going on," one spoke to the other.

"Yes. You said it". The two talked a little about the last week. There they were in the exit and had met some light girls. They wanted to separate to do their rounds when they were surprised. Suddenly, they heard something. It was like a sigh blowing through the hall.

"Did you hear that too?" one asked the other.

"Yes. It must come from the ship". The two slowly stepped towards this one. The other two soldiers also came towards them. They had also heard it.

"What was that?" one asked.

"I don't know," said another. The assault rifles had taken them up and unlocked them. A cold shiver of fear ran down one of the soldiers' backs.

"It's better if we report this," one spoke quietly.

"Yes. Do that," whispered another. The soldier turned around and wanted to leave when something happened. The dragon ship, still wet from the ice water, lit up. It was as if lightning had struck it. The soldiers turned to avoid being blinded. It was only for a moment. Then the light went out. The soldiers looked at the ship again. It looked the same as before but something had changed.

"Look at that!" said one soldier. The other three came closer to the ship and the comrade.

"The water," the man said, "The water is no longer there. It looks as if this light has dried the ship. The ground is also dry".

"You are right. It doesn't smell so damp anymore either".

The third soldier turned around "I'll make the report," he spoke and walked away.

Chapter 49

Professor!" someone shouted. A soldier stood at the professor's door and knocked on the door. The professor was still awake and was reading a book. When he heard the knock, he stood up and walked to the door.

"Professor," called the soldier. "Open the door". He kept banging on the door.

"That's enough. I'm coming out already". The man opened the door and listened to what the soldier wanted from him.

"Come to the hall fast," he said.

"What's the matter?" he asked.

"You will see when you get there". Then the soldier turned around and ran away. The professor didn't lose any time. He informed his assistant and Frank Waldon. The three rushed to the hall a few minutes later. They were received by Sergeant Rock, who had also been taken out of bed.

"So," the professor addressed the sergeant. "What excitement is there here? Why did they get us out of bed?"

"Four of my men were on duty when they suddenly heard a noise that didn't fit here. It was more of a sigh. Then, the ship lit up in a bright light briefly. This is the result". He pointed to the ship.

"Unbelievable!" said the professor.

"That cannot be possible," said Frank Walden.

"Stanley, do you see it?"

"Yes. Everything is dry. All the wood, the supports, the ship, everything's dry".

"How is that possible?" Jeff Dicks said.

"I don't know. But I suspect something," the professor said.

"What?". The sergeant asked the question.

"I guess maybe I have too much imagination, but I think this ship wants us to investigate it".

At first, the sergeant thought that the professor might have been drunk. But, something in him said that he might have been right. "Alright," he said. "Let's delve into the matter". He called for a soldier to bring him the ladder. It was placed on the left side wall.

The sergeant said, "Who wants to be the first?".

The two men, Prof. Dr. Stanley Poken and Frank Waldon, looked at each other. "You, go first," the professor addressed his friend.

"Why me? You were the first one to discover it".

"Yes, but you are the expert on the Drakken".

"Thank you, my friend".

Frank Waldon slowly climbed the steps. It was a strange feeling to be the first to board this rare ship. He had arrived at the end of the steps and was looking down. There, the other men were gathered. There was no turning back. He swung his leg over the railing and placed it on the wooden planks. 'What a strange feeling,' he thought. He pulled his other leg and stood on holy ground. Subsequently, he thought at that moment. Slowly, without damaging anything, he moved towards the middle of the ship. There was the strange construction of a wooden roof. Since it came from the stern, it had to overcome a few steps before it was there. 'I hope the wood is under my feet,' he thought. The wood withstood his weight. It was as if the ship had never been in the ice. Uncertain and full of curiosity, he stood in front of the wooden construction. He just looked at it. Then his fingers stroked, somehow tenderly, over the wood. It was warm. 'Strange,' he thought. 'How is such a thing possible?'. He didn't think much about it, he just wanted to solve the mystery and looked at the wooden house from all sides. On the bow side, he came across a door. That was because the cracks were clearly visible.

"A door's here!" he shouted down.

"What?!" the professor shouted up.

Frank spoke, "A door!" again. He bent over the railing. "It leads into the wooden roof. I'll try to open it".

"Should I send someone up there to help you?"

"Not necessarily. I'll be fine". Then, he turned away and stood in front of the door again. With a chisel that he always carries with him, he gently poked into the cracks to remove the dirt that had accumulated over the last centuries. When he finished, after a good quarter of an hour, he breathed deeply. Then he pressed against the wooden door. It gave way and fell inside. When it hit the door, the wooden floor vibrated. It was so heavy. Frank reached back and pulled a flashlight out of the pocket he had put in before. He turned it on as he stepped inside with a bad feeling. The cone of light found its way. Frank shone the inside of this wooden canopy to the furthest corner. At the back, there were some wooden boxes. He wanted to look at them. Slowly, he moved towards them and when he was in the middle, it happened. The wooden floor gave way and he fell into the hull of the ship. He screamed quietly in horror. When he hit the ground, he couldn't find his way around. Fortunately, he had a flashlight. Subsequently, he could orientate himself. It lay next to him and shines somewhere. He lifted it up, looked around and understood nothing more. Such ships did not have such a large cavity.

'What a bizarre ship,' he thought. With the flashlight, he shone it into the rounds. What he saw was fascinating. The whole cavity was full of wooden boxes. But these were not lying horizontally on the floor. Instead, they stood vertically. The size of these boxes was already impressive. Frank Waldon was no small man. But these boxes almost towered over him by two heads. He estimated them at over two meters. The width was also considerable. He did not understand all that. 'Are these…coffins?' he thought. Curiosity had gripped him. He wanted to see what was inside. With the chisel, he tried to open the wooden box. Which he also succeeded. The flashlight was stuck between his lips as he opened one side of the wooden box. Frank Waldon put it aside and took the flashlight out of his mouth. He now held it in his right hand. The ray of light was directed at the inside of the box. What Frank saw at that moment was incredible. The wooden box was not empty. In it, stood a human figure. It was a Viking. Frank hadn't expected that. The stranger had a beard and had his hands crossed in front of his chest. He wore iron rings around his fingers and a decorated metal belt on his belly. The headgear consisted of an iron helmet with two horns. Under his helmet, long, dark blonde hair came to light. They were pulled together towards the bottom. He looked into the Viking's face and recognized it. It was the first face on the ship's wood. He wanted to take a closer look at this person and took a step forward. Frank's heart beat wildly. He hadn't expected that here. This was the discovery of the millennium, and he was the first to see it. Even so, he had a strange feeling. The air down here was kind of strange.

'If here, in this box, there is a Viking, then in the other boxes must be…' He couldn't finish thinking the thought because he was terrified. The Viking had opened his eyes wide and looked at him viciously. Frank Waldon backed away and screamed out his fear terribly.

Chapter 50

The sergeant was getting impatient downstairs. "Mr. Waldon surely takes his time," said Sergeant Rock.

"He is like that. He wants to take a close look at everything," the professor said. But he had to admit to himself that Frank took his time. Something was wrong and his forehead frowned. 'If Frank doesn't notice he's taking so long, then I'll have to climb up,' he thought. Moments later, he knew he had to do it. All present heard a terrible scream.

"Frank!" the professor shouted. A shiver ran down his back. The same happened to the others.

"Go quickly!" the sergeant called out to two soldiers. They rushed over and ran up the steps.

"What is going on here?!" someone shouted from behind. It was General Cobe. He had been informed by Sergeant Rock a few minutes ago.

"We heard a scream from inside the ship, Sir. It's Mr. Waldon in there."

"Get him out. Now!".

"Two men are already up, Sir," he told the general.

"Then, why is it taking so long?" he said.

"I don't know, Sir".

Moments later, three men appeared at the railing. It was the two soldiers and Frank Waldon. He had to be supported, because he was weakened by the shock he had received. The two soldiers helped him to overcome the height. On the ground, the other men received the man and laid him down. A glass of water was brought to him. He was also examined by a doctor who had come. Slowly, Frank's wit returned to normal.

"Frank," the professor spoke to his friend. "What happened?". He swallowed and breathed deeply.

He just said, "They're alive".

"What happened?" the general asked the two soldiers who had taken him out. They stood tight in front of their general.

"Sir. We went inside and saw this man in the ship's hull. When he saw us, he stretched out his hands towards us. We grabbed him and pulled him up. That is all, Sir". The man looked at them and nodded.

"Kick it". The two stepped aside and joined the other soldiers. Frank had gotten back on his feet.

"Subsequently, what was going on in there?" the general wanted to know. The question was burning in everyone present. Frank told the men. When he was finished with the story, even the general swallowed.

"You mean to believe there are more Vikings in all those other boxes?"

"I'm convinced of that."

"I'm thinking about sending someone in or not".

"To do what?" asked Frank Waldon.

"To get the boxes out".

"I would advise against that".

"Why?"

"I think I hinted them off. The Viking who awoke will surely get the others out of the boxes. When the time comes, they will come out on their own".

"Hmm..." the man started to absorb and think. 'How could we go on, then?' General Cobe thought. 'What happens when these men come out'.

"There is only one way to receive these Vikings properly," he said.

"And that would be," asked Prof. Dr. Stanley Poken, "The man who is the last to be seen in the line of ancestors".

He turned to Sergeant Rock and looked at his wristwatch. "It's almost eleven o'clock. Fly away now. Get me that Fenton".

"Yes, Sir". He greeted and disappeared from the men's field of vision.

Chapter 51

In the vastness of the universe, a signal from the earth's parabolic antennas shot as a bright beam through. It was Erik's scream that penetrated the dark universe. The devastating scream passed countless black holes and stars till it reached a galaxy zillions of light-years away from Earth.

In the planet Zeres, great creatures once lived. Their technology and power were far superior to the humans. But on modern times, these people did not exist anymore because an ominous war had taken place. Over a thousand years ago, a foreign, malicious race attacked the planet. The houses and everything on them were blazed to the ground. Even the bacteria and microbes had not survived. The planet had become a sandy desert. In some places, the planet accumulated large, over-sized holes. But the debris from the holes did not completely disappear into space. It floated and formed as a large ring around the planet. The ring looked like the Saturn of the Solar system. There were dust particles, stones, and thousands of tiny black square metal boxes. They weren't only as they appear to be, though. It was waiting for a signal - a specific scream. And it came!

One of the small boxes caught the signal and a light shone immediately inside. The small box passed the signal on to the other metal boxes. Soon, all boxes lit up. Then, they came out of the ring and floated towards the planet. There, they gathered. A cylinder came out of one side of each box, while a hole was made on the other side. It was a chain reaction when the boxes merged into one big box. As soon as they were together, there was a pitch-black flash of energy. It covered the whole cube. The square box rose and floated above the ground. It did not float far, just enough to reach the metal post that protruded from the ground. The box lowered over the post and covered it. The black source of energy flowed into the ground and vanished. Moments later, the ground began to vibrate and tremble. A quake of enormous proportions was the result.

Fissures opened and the black energy, as well as hot, dark steam shot up like a fountain. The cracks became bigger and bigger. The ground opened and a huge black spaceship came out of the ground. Stones and sand were thrown away when it was completely out of the ground. As soon as it had flown a few meters above the ground, it set course. It looked for the origin of the signal. As soon as the spacecraft was outside the planet, black thorns shot from the spacecraft to the planet. They anchored themselves to the planet's surface. Then, a dark beam of energy from the spaceship shot towards the spikes. They caught him and sent him underground. There, in the core, it united. The planet Zeres did not exist anymore in a matter of seconds. It exploded. Meteorites shot through space as dangerous projectiles. Meanwhile, the spaceship was already at a safe distance and flew out into the vastness of space.

Chapter 52

Outside the small town was the Saranac Lake. Erik Fenton had retreated to this part of the wilderness. The log cabin stood towards the lake. Behind it the Whiteface Mountains towered up. Erik lay on the bed and slept very bad that night. He kept turning around on both sides. Once he lay on his back and later on his stomach. He blinked as he reached for the alarm clock with his left hand. He was standing on the bedside table next to the bed. Erik pressed a button and the indicator light showed him the time. 'Two o'clock,' he thought. He turned back to his side and tried to fall asleep, which he succeeded in doing. But it didn't last long, because he woke up again. In this wilderness, he knew every sound of nature. But this time, it was something else that brought him out of his sleep. It was a flutter that got closer and louder. Erik stood up and moved to the window. Despite the darkness, he now realized what had gotten him out of bed. It was a helicopter.

The flight lights on the runners flashed as he landed on the meadow behind the log cabin. Then, the engines were turned off. The rotors were still spinning a little, until peace returned in this area. The side door of the helicopter opened and three men got out. The pilot of the helicopter remained seated in the pulpit. The three men moved towards the log cabin and stopped in front of it. They waited until the back door was opened. Erik Fenton, who had dressed quickly, stepped out. Above the door, a small lamp shone. He looked at the three men. They were soldiers. One of them had the rank of a sergeant. The other two were under his command. They carried automatic rapid-fire rifles. They pointed to the ground. Erik didn't trust them because they could be lifted quickly and kill him if they insist. That's why his right hand was behind his back. There was a handgun in his waistband. He was willing to use it if he felt threatened.

The sergeant took one, then, a second step forward. "Mr. Fenton," he addressed the man. "Mr. Erik Fenton?"

"Who wants to know?"

"Sergeant Rock. US Army. Fort Tilden. New York".

"I am Erik Fenton. What's a sergeant from New York doing here at this hour?"

"You."

"Well, now that you've found me, what do you want from me?"

"We need you to accompany us".

"Where to?"

"To New York. I got the order from General Cobe to fly you to New York".

"General Cobe? Never heard of him. Why does he want to see me?"

"Because he wants an answer from you".

"What does he want an answer to?". Fenton was tired of this question and answer game.

"General Cobe wants to know how your face got on the dragon ship," the sergeant answered.

Erik staggered back a little. He felt queasy in his stomach when he heard the word. He regained his composure, although he didn't want it to be true. "The dragon! The warriors! Are they there?"

"They seem to know something, don't they?"

He nodded before pronouncing "My God."

"What have you got?" asked Sergeant Rock.

"What do I have? I may have conjured up death."

"Whose death? Yours?"

"If only it were just me. But I'm afraid it is, perhaps, the downfall of this world".

The sergeant swallowed. "So bad?" he whispered. He was no longer well in his skin.

"Maybe even worse. But I will do everything to prevent it. Take me to General Cobe and the Dragon Ship". His right hand detached itself from the weapon grip. He took it forward. Minutes later, the helicopter rotated again. Erik was already sitting when the sergeant sat next to him. "How did you find me?" he asked.

"Through the files of Tom Stone and through our radios," said the Sergeant. Sergeant Rock had to talk louder because the noise was evident inside the helicopter.

"I called the Sheriff of Saranac Lake during the flight here. He didn't seem particularly pleased when I got him out of bed. Still, he gave me the exact place where you are and I found you". Inside the flying machine, there were five men sitting who kept silent and flew to Fort Tilden.

Chapter 53

A dark light lit up aboard the spacecraft. Some lamps of the equipment lit up. In a special wing, there were countless pressurized cabins. They stood vertically and something was moving in them. The pressure was automatically released and the cabins opened. Disgusting creatures stepped out. Since there was almost no light in the room, you could only see the contours of the creatures. One of these hideous creatures hissed something at the other. "Our treacherous brother has betrayed us."

"Yes," the other hissed "And he must die for his deed". The other creatures moved towards the control systems of the spaceship. There they saw where the signal had come from and followed it unnoticed.

Chapter 54

Three days ago. Kalish had been in hiding for over three weeks. Despite the police's nationwide search, he remained untraceable. He had settled down with a friend from days gone by. The gunshot wound on his right leg was still burning a little. However, the hatred for this cop continued to be ablaze. In the past few days, he had been on the phone to the Middle East. Kalish had a friend there who owed him a favor.

"Listen," he said. "I need two of your best men".

"Why do you need them?"

"Don't ask questions. Just send them here".

"Alright. What day do you need them?"

"They have to be here in three days". Kalish told the friend where to meet.

"They will be there. Consider the favor I owed you redeemed". Then, the alleged friend broke the line.

Chapter 55

The two men arrived that day. Kalish had instructed his friend who was just staying with the two men to pick them up at the airport. They were thoroughly examined at customs. The luggage, their bodies—everything. Then, they were allowed to pass. Outside, they were received and picked up by Kalish's friend. They drove to the apartment where he waited for them and greeted them. Then, he put firearms he had gotten them before into their hands and said, "On that night, the cop will lose something".

"What? His life?" He was asked.

"Of course. But before that, someone else must die first".

Chapter 56

Fort Tilden. Half past five in the morning. The hall was in a state of alarm. Several soldiers stood in a row around the dragon ship. They aimed their rapid-fire rifles at it as ordered by the general. It was the general who addressed the professor. "Do you hear anything?"

The professor had pressed his face against the ship's side and listened. "I hear noises," he said.

"My God!" Frank Waldon whispered. "They're awake".

"You may be right, my friend". The professor moved away from the ship's wall. "It's better to keep your distance. You never know". The men stepped behind the soldier line.

"Now, let's wait and see," said Frank Waldon. The tension increased. None of those present knew when anything might or what was actually happening.

An hour later, one of the soldiers called out to his comrades. "There! Something is moving up there". Everyone looked up.

"Actually," the professor whispered. A big figure came out of the inside and stood at the railing. In his right hand, he held a huge axe. Around his decorated belt, he also carried a short sword and a knife. "This is the Viking I saw," Frank whispered to the others. The colossus raised his right arm and growled. The axe flashed in artificial lamplight.

The general shouted to his soldiers, "Nobody shoots!". Although, most of the soldiers' fingers were already itchy. The figure lowered her arm and turned around. Behind the Viking, there appeared other Nordic warriors. "My God!" said the general. "There are so many". Over fifty Vikings came out of the ship's belly. Each one was armed. They looked at the strangely dressed men standing in a row at the bottom. The warriors waited for a sign from their leader. He saw the ladder standing at the railing. Since it was forgotten by the soldiers, the big figure took this way down. He took one step at a time and climbed the stairs to reach the solid ground. The Viking took two steps forward and stopped. With his left hand, he waved to his warriors. One by one, they came down the ladder and stopped next to their leader.

"It is better if one of us would dare to go forward," whispered the professor.

"General," Frank Waldon asked, "Are you going?"

"Why me? You are the general here". Frank Waldon shook his head. 'He's a general, has earned the stars in his uniform and doesn't have the courage,' he thought.

"It would be better if we welcome them with friendship," said Jeff Dicks. The assistant was right.

Frank Waldon took the first step, then the second. He passed the soldiers' line and stopped three steps in front of the giant figure. First, he cleared his throat before he began to speak. "Welcome!" he just said and spread out his arms. He wanted to make it clear to the warriors that they were welcome. Although he knew that these Vikings could not understand or speak American. But somehow, he had to say something. Then he took his arms down again. He raised his right arm again and knocked his hand against his chest. "Me Frank," he said. "Frank".

The giant warrior growled and raised his right arm. With the axe, he pointed upwards. In the direction where his face was drawn on the ship. With his left hand, he pointed against himself. He spoke, "Erik," with a thundering voice. Frank Waldon and the others were surprised when they heard a name.

"I understood him," Prof. Dr. Poken whispered to the general.

"He speaks our language," said the general.

"I wouldn't conclude language," contradicted Jeff Dicks. "He only mentioned his name". The assistant was right with his statement.

"He will talk much more once I talk to him," someone behind the men spoke. They turned around and saw two men coming at them. One was Sergeant Rock. The other no less than Erik Fenton. Both had landed on the premises a few minutes ago. The sergeant had informed Erik Fenton with what he knew. The former cop stepped towards the men. They stepped aside and let him through. His eyes were not on the scientists nor the general. It only saw the warriors before them. He stopped in front of the colossus of the Vikings and looked at him. He raised his right arm and pointed his finger upwards. That must be his face engraved. He only spoke "Erik," and pointed at himself. "I am the first," said the Viking.

"I am the last," Fenton said.

"He talks," the general whispered to the others.

"Psst!" the professor called him. Everyone wanted to hear something. But what they wanted most of all, was to understand what the two discusses with each other.

"Son of the sons of my sons. Why did this happen? Why did you wake us up?"

Erik knew that this Viking was his ancestor. "I was tortured. The pain was unbearable. I wanted to die so that you would find eternal peace. But now, I cannot undo it".

The Viking nodded. "Who was it who inflicted pain on you?"

"It was a man named Kalish. He escaped that day. Nobody knows where he is right now."

"We will find out". He took a short break before continuing, "You have something with you. Give it to me". Erik knew what it was. He took it out of his jacket pocket and gave it to him.

"What is it?" the general asked the sergeant.

"No idea. It looks like a metallic cylinder". Erik gave the cylinder to the

Viking. The colossus also brought something out under his fur clothing. It was the counterpart. He put both together.

"Are you ready for this journey?" asked the Viking.

"Journey? What journey are you talking about?"

"The journey to the land of our fathers. You will learn how to fight there".

"I can take care of myself very well," said Erik.

"But if the Ungudds show up here, you have to face them with your blade. Otherwise, you'll never be able to kill them".

Frank Waldon had slowly stepped back to the others and listened carefully to the Viking's words. He could only understand a fraction of what the giant warrior said.

"What is he saying?" asked his friend. The general also wanted to know.

"Who are these Ungudds?"

"They are evil spirits," Frank whispered to them.

The other warriors looked at Erik Fenton who nodded. "I am ready to go with you". That was the moment when something occurred. The cylinder in the Viking's hand began to glow. The light in the hall flickered. Erik's body began to glow, enveloping him, and he wasn't the only one. The other Vikings bathed in the mysterious light at the same time.

"Stand back!" the general ordered the soldiers. They stepped backwards. In their hands, they held the rapid-fire rifles. It was more a security for themselves. Those present watched as the warriors disintegrated in a bright light of lightning. Before that, Erik Fenton looked back and shouted something to the men, "I saw the future! Evacuate all people from New York!". Then he disappeared. He disintegrated like the Vikings. The place where he had stood before became empty. The general did not understand how something like this could happen.

"You heard what he said," the professor said to General Cobe.

"I heard it. But what and how should I explain it to the others at the Pentagon or maybe to the President?"

"That's your problem. I believe Erik Fenton. When he says that we should go away, then we must go away," said the professor.

"I understand," said General Cobe and breathed deeply. "I will make sure everything will happen". Minutes later, he was gone to another place.

Chapter 57

Helen Turner slept bad that night. She didn't know why, but she thought of Erik Fenton. She opened her eyes briefly and looked at the alarm clock. It was on the dresser. It showed to be about five o'clock in the morning. 'Too early to get up,' she thought and rolled to the side. She wanted to sleep a little further. Since the bedroom door was open, she immediately heard the noise at the front door. 'Is someone outside?' she thought. She stood up and slowly walked forward. Her senses were tense. 'Who could it be this early?' was her thought. She wore a dressing gown over her nightgown. Her feet stuck on her comfortable furry slippers. She crossed the corridor as quiet as she could, and stopped at the front door. She wanted to look through the peephole to see who was standing in front of the door, but she didn't get to that anymore. The front door came towards her. Someone had kicked the door so it opened inside. Helen screamed as the front door hit her face. She staggered backwards and fell down. She didn't see who was entering her apartment at that moment. According to the footsteps, there had to be more than one person. Her nose hurt and bled as she stood up. With a hazy vision, she saw a face above her. When this face began to speak, her imminent fear arose again. "Hello, sweetheart. Do you still remember me?".

She shouted, "No! Go away!" to the male voice. She waved her arms back and forth to free herself from this man.

"That won't do you any good. Get up". She was packed in her dressing gown and pulled up. Helen now recognized exactly who else were in the apartment. There were two more men there. One of them had closed the front door again. The other stood to the left of the man. Both had firearms in their hands. Helen's gaze had briefly touched both, but her exact gaze was on the guy in front of her.

"Kalish, you..." she said.

"You remember my name? That's nice. Because that name will burn into your brain till you die".

"Why are you doing all this? I am not important to you, at all".

"Yes, you are. You are friends with the fuckin' cop and that already says everything". He grabbed her hard, pulled her into the living room and threw her there on an armchair.

"You'll remain seated. If you get up, then…you already know what happens next!" Then, Kalish turned away. He talked to the other two in a foreign language. These nodded. Then he turned to Helen. "The air is clear. No one has yet noticed our intrusion. But, where's the cop?"

"I don't know," she said full of fear.

"You'll tell me, or should I do with you what I did with him?"

"I really don't know". Her heart was racing. The breath was heavy. This devil would only let her go once he had killed her.

"All right. You wanted it that way". He hissed something to the two others. One came towards Kalish. He had a bag with him and reached into it. He pulled out an adhesive tape and handed it to Kalish. This dangerous man pulled up the tape and wrapped Helen in her armchair. She couldn't move anymore. Then, he detached a piece of the tape and taped her mouth shut. "Let's see if you still won't talk later." Helen didn't feel well. Her nose was bleeding. The sticky lifeblood ran down her throat over the tape. Add to this the fear she felt. "You will tell me where he is". Kalish took some toothpicks from his pocket. "Look what I have here". Helen reared in fear. She had a lot of respect for these toothpicks. "Well? Where is he?". She nodded and he understood. With a jerky move, he tore the tape from her mouth. "So? What do you have to say to me?"

"He...he's not here. He's in Saranac Lake".

"Do you have his phone number?"

"He doesn't have a phone there. But the number of his cell phone is in my notebook". Helen was ashamed that she had to give out his whereabouts and phone number.

"Good girl," spoke Kalish. He got the notebook and flew over the pages. He immediately discovered the number, grabbed the phone and dialed it. "The line is dead," he commented in surprise. Then, he put the handset on the fork and turned to Helen Turner. "Well, if he's not there, then I'll have some fun with you". He took a toothpick in his hand and approached her. The fear came up in her.

She screamed out her lover's name loudly, "Erik!".

"No. Kalish is my name. I will kill you if you get it wrong, bitch". But it came quite different than Kalish hoped.

Chapter 58

Erik, his ancestor and the other Vikings proceeded on their journey. It was the journey to a place he did not know. The light, surrounded the men, became weaker and disappeared shortly afterwards. Erik looked around and saw mountains and lakes. "These are the fjords in which we once lived," said the Viking.

"Beautiful," Erik gave his comment and looked at everything carefully. He liked it here. Suddenly the ancestor spoke to him.

"You mentioned earlier that a man named Kalish forced you to scream".

"Yes. What about him?"

"I feel some kind of connection. Are you united with someone?" Erik thought about it. There was only one person. It was not his Mother. But it was Helen Turner.

"Yes, she is the woman I love".

"Don't you feel it, too?" asked the Viking. Erik listened to himself and realized that his ancestor was right. Someone thought of him. It was Helen. Suddenly, he had a vision. He saw Helen threatened by three men. One of them was Kalish. He closed his eyes and heard Helen call his name. She screamed in fear. Erik opened his eyes.

"She is in danger! I have to go to her".

"You don't have to go yourself," said the Viking. "I will go. You stay here". As soon as he had said this, he disappeared right before Erik's eyes. The light had enveloped him and left the place empty where he had just stood. Erik prayed that his ancestor would arrive in time.

Chapter 59

Something's wrong here," said one of the two men in Helen Turner's apartment. He was the one standing next to the front door. He lifted up his gun and released it. Kalish shouted to him, "What is it?!"

"I don't know. The air smells so different here".

"Yes," the other one answered. "I'm not sure either".

"Oh, nonsense! You must be dreaming. Have you taken anything for yourself?" Kalish turned to his victim. He already wanted to torture her when he smelled it too. It was a smell he had smelled some time ago. That was in the old warehouse. "I smell it too. Get ready," he told the two of them. As soon as he said it, there was a bang and the front door was pushed in. The door fell off its hinges and rumbled to the floor. One guy at the door took himself to safety with one sentence. Then, he lifted the gun and turned it against the door cutout. There stood a creature he didn't know. The contours of the Being shone. It was a strangely dressed man and, in his hand, he held a huge axe. The man pulled the trigger and another one mingled in his shot. The other guy had also seen the man and pulled the trigger. The shots sounded too loud in the house. Both bullets hit the Viking. But they bounced off the fluctuating light. It was as if the Viking had an unseen bulletproof vest.

The Viking growled loudly and threw himself forward. More shots fell in his scream. He screamed, "Odin!" when one guy collapsed dead under the force of the axe. The second man was in the same situation. He split him in two halves. Both died a quick death. Then, the Viking moved into the living room and saw the woman sitting in the armchair. A man stood behind her and held a knife to her throat. Helen didn't know who scares her more. Kalish or from this colossus who appeared out of nowhere? The Viking approached both of them.

"Not a step further," Kalish said. "Or she dies". The Viking stopped. His axe pointed to the ground. The blood of the other two men ran down it. The red drops mixed on the carpet to form a stain.

"Because of your fault, you woke me and my men. Through your guilt, many will find death. But you... You will find it today and now".

"I don't believe you! I decide what happens here". Kalish felt safe. He only had to pull the knife through the woman's throat and climb out of the window. There was a fire escape. But the Viking didn't let him any time with his plan. His light-clad figure changed. The light became brighter. Then, lightning shot out of his body and hit Kalish. He couldn't even do anything. He tilted backwards and stayed lying. His body was paralyzed. He saw the colossus coming towards him and stopping next to him.

"How small you look," the Viking remarked, mockingly. "As small as an ant. I like insects that do something for nature. But there are others, the Vermins, that destroy everything. I like to crush them. You are one of them". The Viking lifted his heavy foot and pressed it on the chest of this terrorist. The crackling could not be overheard. The giant broke the man many ribs. Kalish screamed devastatingly. The pain was unbearable.

"How does it feel?" said the Viking. "Can you bear the pain?" Kalish didn't cry out any more. The Viking raised his axe. Then he slashed it down, putting an end to Kalish and separated his head from the torso. Then, he turned away and immediately stood in front of the woman. Helen didn't know what to do. She wanted to run away. But the tape kept holding her in the armchair. She was afraid of this Viking. The giant Colossus growled as he looked at her. "It's over now," he just said, pulling out his knife and cutting the tape in two. "I have to go now. Erik, your friend, is waiting for me". The Viking walked to the door. Before he walked through it, he turned around.

"Leave this part of the city. Go to where Erik was last seen. Only then, when everything is over, you can come back".

"Where is Erik?" she asked. But a light had formed around the Viking. He disappeared before Helen's eyes. As soon as he was gone, Helen ran to the telephone. There she called Tom Stone.

When the captain arrived from the 70th precinct, he found Helen

Turner on the ground. She had fainted because the shock was too deep. Blood was spread all over the floor and three corpses were lying in it. Tom Stone whispered, "My God! Helen Turner will have to explain some things to us when she wakes up".

Chapter 60

In front of Erik Fenton's eyes, the area began to flicker. Erik, the Viking, had appeared again. Erik Fenton saw blood on his axe. The Viking noticed this and calmed him down. "It is the blood of Kalish and his friends. He won't harm anyone anymore".

"And Helen?"

"Your woman is fine. I told her to go to the place where you were before".

"How do you know where I was?" asked Erik.

"From the Light. From the Nameless one. He knows a lot".

"I also want to know, because I also have a part of him in me".

"Patience. First, we will stay here for a while and prepare you for the fight. Then, I will tell you everything".

Chapter 61

It was 9'oclock in the morning at the Pentagon. The Crisis team came together. High generals and security guards sat together in the conference room. Everyone had a seat at the large oval table. General Cobe had ordered a meeting. "We shall, what?!" shouted one of the other generals.

"Evacuate New York," Cobe said.

"We can't do that if we don't have solid evidence on why we should do it. You can't just evacuate an entire city after a word from a man who appeared out of nowhere," another said.

"There would be panic among the population," another said.

"I understand your doubts gentlemen. I also doubted, but now I believe this man. Take a look at the files I put down for you. You will see why".

"How do you picture that in front of General Cobe? Shall we go out on the street and tell people to leave their homes just because we suspect ancient ghosts would come here?"

"No. Ungudds," said another.

"Yes. I also read that in the report," said a third. Everyone spoke in a confused way. Everyone gave their opinion. General Cobe knew that it would be difficult to convince the others. But he did not let it get him down. He struck the tabletop with his hand.

"Enough!" he called into the round. "We have to decide. Here and now".

"Well, I'm against it," one said.

"Me, too," said another. Some raised their hands in the air.

"That's your answer," General Cobe asked in the round.

"It looks that way," said one.

"Not so fast," said another. The man who said this was still reading the report. He was bent forward. Only now, did he lean back.

"General Cobe. I was reading your report. It is very revealing. But there is one little thing missing".

"And that would be?"

"I'll talk about it in a moment. But first, I would like to repeat what the report says. Subsequently, we have a man named Erik Fenton. He was a former cop in New York. He is connected to the dragon ship which was buried in an iceberg. He also has a connection with the crew of the dragon ship. With living Vikings who have dissolved with this Erik Fenton in a mysterious light source. The report also states that this Fenton had already had contact with a 'light' a few weeks ago. That was in an abandoned warehouse at the port".

"That's what it says in the report," said General Cobe.

"But what is not in the report that is important is…," said the man. He fetched a report from his briefcase which stood next to his armchair. "Here, gentlemen," he began, "I have a report from New Mexico. I got this message from the head of the research institute after the search of extraterrestrial life form. A Jack Clark was on duty that night. He reported that he had heard a scream which had penetrated into the headquarters. This cry, or a signal, left Earth via radio telescopes. This happened a few minutes after this Erik Fenton had contact with the Light".

"This is very interesting," said a senior officer.

"That's it, and it goes on. I got another message on the day the Iceberg was spotted in Greenland. This happened almost at the same time.

Subsequently, gentlemen. I believe that Erik Fenton and these Vikings didn't come together just like that. They are here because of the Ungudds. These Ungudds or evil spirits, as the Vikings called them, are actually Beings from another world, or so it appears to be".

"Aliens, you mean?" someone asked.

"That's what I mean and we should believe General Cobe and this Fenton". It was as quiet in the round as in a cemetery. Nobody wanted to say anything. Suddenly, the phone rang. Someone in security picked up and listened to the voice.

"It's for you, General Cobe" the man said. The general stepped up to the phone and listened to the voice. Then he hooked up the phone and went to his seat. "That was," he started "Sergeant Rock. A good soldier and my confidante. He told me that a bright light was seen by a New York resident. But that's not all. One of the Vikings was active. He was in Helen Turner's apartment. She is Mr. Fenton's girlfriend. The Viking caused a bloodbath".

"The woman is dead?" one asked.

"No! Three men died. Three men from the Middle East, to be exact. They tried to kill the woman. One of them was the outlaw Kalish, which you, gentlemen, have read in the report".

"It seems to me that these Vikings are targeting evil," said a head of security.

"You may be right in there," said General Cobe before continuing. "Did you see the colossus and can hold it?"

"No, he disappeared".

"Well, gentlemen, what does the situation look like now that other, new facts have been presented to us? Can we now begin with the evacuation of New York?"

One said, "It's a difficult decision".

"It is better if we have the support of the President," said another.

"Good! I'll do that," General Cobe said.

"I will accompany them," said the man who had helped him. A little later, they were on their way to the president.

Chapter 62

Evacuate New York?!" shouted the president. "Are you out of your mind? That is out of the question".

"With all due respect, Sir. May I ask why not? The facts are in front of you," Cobe said.

"That's simple. As long as I don't have proof of an extraterrestrial attack, I can't do that. Nevertheless, I wanted to meet you. Prevention is everything. Our armed forces should just remain on high alert. You, General Cobe, are authorized by me to set everything in motion".

"Thank you, Sir!". The two men said goodbye to the President and left the White House.

Chapter 63

New Mexico. It was night. Jack Clark sat in his chair and looked at the computer screen. He had his feet on the table and rocked the chair. His supervisor had been instructed by the authorities to pay attention to everything that was moving in space. The supervisor had passed this instruction on to his colleagues. That night, Jack Clark shoved a quiet bullet. 'Nothing is happening anyway,' he thought. His gaze was tied to the monitor and this changed. The instruments started to work. It was like the night when he heard the scream. "Damn!" he shouted full of horror and immediately an "Ouch," came over his lips. He had tipped backwards and hit the ground. He stood up and sounded the alarm. He put the chair back into position and sat down on it. His superior came running to him.

"What is it?" he asked.

"I got a signal," Jack said. "It's weak, but it's a signal".

"Proximity?"

"Between Mars and Jupiter".

"But there are no satellites there".

"Maybe an Explorer satellite on its way to Jupiter?"

"Possible," said the superior. "It is possible that he transmitted the message to the other satellites". The two looked at the monitor to see something.

"There!" said Jack Clark and pointed his finger at the screen. "Right there. You see that, too, right?"

"Yes. I see it". A round spot appeared on the screen.

"Incredible," Jack said. "How can you overcome a vast distance so quickly?"

"Only those who are in the round thing knows that," said the superior. Then he hurried to the phone and passed the message on to the Pentagon.

Chapter 64

At first, the New Yorkers thought it was a joke when the president declared a state of emergency. But when the National Guard convened and arrived with trucks, guns, tanks, and the anti-aircraft guns, some realized it was no joke. Millions of people immediately left New York in panic. The streets were crowded with cars and buses. Everyone wanted to get away from there as quickly as possible. It was utter chaos. It was like someone at the Pentagon had said and anticipated. Recalcitrant were shot by the soldiers. The blood of the dead dried in the sun.

After three days, the streets were deserted. Paper sheets, garbage bags, broken bicycles, motorcycles and demolished cars were everywhere. Some people who did not want to leave stayed in their houses. John F. Kennedy International Airport and La Guardia Airport were closed to commercial aircrafts. Only military planes were allowed to take off and land. Special combat helicopters with heavy weapons stood in a waiting position. Just as fast jets of the most modern air force stood, at the edge of the runway, in a row. Each of the fighter pilots waited for the mission. Now the long and uncertain waiting began.

Chapter 65

On board the spacecraft, many lights lit up and down. The hideous creatures stood at the controls and navigated their spaceship towards Earth. "Our brother hid here," said one creature.

"Yes. His cry came from here," said another one. He pointed to some lights that lit up in front of the Being. One point was New York.

"What are these living Beings that live here?" asked one Being another.

"From the star charts, they are humans. A primitive people who like to destroy themselves."

"Never mind. That won't do our brother any good. He will not escape us this time and definitely not those who help him," another Being next to the two announced himself. Slowly and without haste the spaceship approached the earth's atmosphere. Then, it penetrated and came closer to America.

Chapter 66

There was a mess in the world. Each nation tried to make contact with the spaceship and got no connection. People who were afraid fled the cities. It was worse than in New York and nobody knew what to do next.

There was no civilization in the wilderness of the Fjords. There was no electricity or houses as they were known. However, there were only a few wooden huts here and Erik lived with the Vikings in them. He didn't have to worry much about the food because these men knew how to get it. The drinking water gushed from a small stream not far from the huts to Tale. Erik Fenton had taken off his clothes and put on the same clothes as the Vikings. He had found them in one of the wooden huts. His appearance had also changed. He let his beard grow because he could not shave. Since the first day of his arrival, he had received the sword from his ancestor. He has to learn how to handle it. In the beginning, it was very difficult to lift this thing. But with time, it became lighter and Erik's muscles became stronger. The Vikings had a lot of patience with Erik. Days, even weeks passed until Erik had learned to fight with his sword. One evening, Erik, the Viking, asked Fenton to join him. So did the rest of the Vikings. Everyone sat around a big campfire. Erik sat to the right of his ancestor and looked at him with excitement. He noticed that the Viking wanted to say something. That's why he didn't speak a word and let time pass.

"I see you want to ask me a lot of questions," said Erik, the Viking.

"Yes," said Fenton. "Please take it all in turn".

"Please ask me" and the giant nodded.

"How is it possible that I understand you. How can you speak our language if you've never been in touch with the American or English language, respectively?"

"For my men and me, it was easy to learn your language. In all the centuries when we were in deep sleep, only two had the opportunity to communicate with us. One was the Nameless one. The other was the one who died and his face came on the dragon boat. With this connection, the man's language and knowledge came to us. The Nameless one passed it on to us. Subsequently, we learned the language in deep sleep, because we were connected with this Being".

"Interesting," spoke Fenton.

"What happened next? How did the encounter between the Nameless one and you Vikings come about?"

"The Nameless one could tell you that himself".

"And what?"

"By his power. He would need a few minutes to tell you everything. But for this explanation he would lose part of his power. We still need his strength. Subsequently, I will tell you his and our story". There was a small pause until Erik, the Viking, started with the story of the Nameless.

Chapter 67

New York. Day X had come. The sun darkened. At exactly 11.30 a.m. a huge shadow covered large parts of New York. The shadow wandered on and suddenly stopped. The spaceship that caused the shadow had come to a standstill. After a few minutes it sank and came closer to the ground. The soldiers on the ground had prepared all their guns and were waiting for their general's orders. The men in the tanks and next to the defensive guns were nervous. All had military training and knew how to confront their enemies. But here? They didn't know it against these aliens. That was a new experience.

"Yes, Mr. President," a man spoke into a mobile phone. It was General Cobe. He was behind a protective wall of sandbags and felt so small and tiny.

Soldiers with machine guns stood in front of him. The men's finger twitched. But nobody dared to start, because that could have fatal consequences. "I'll do what I have to do, Sir," Cobe said, breaking the connection. This was bad enough already, because the spaceship sent out unknown signals and disturbed the radio connection of the mobile phone. Cobe he turned to the right.

There stood Sergeant Rock. "As if I had not suspected it".

"You were right, Sir" said Sergeant Rock. "It's awfully amazing that these extraterrestrials came right here. Right here where it all started". The two were in Riverside near Whitestone and stood a little apart from the soldiers. But Sergeant Rock had heard a whisper from two soldiers when he had spoken to the general. The two men, with their weapons in their hands, had spoken despite the absolute ban on speaking.

"This spaceship is enormous. It's like the ID4 movie," said one of the soldiers.

"No, more like in the movie "War of the Worlds," the other said.

Sergeant Rock was quick with both of them. "Keep your fucking mouth shut," he gave the biting order. The two of them fell silent. Then Sergeant Rock stepped back, one by one.

"What's the next step, Sir?"

"No question, we'll—!" General Cobe didn't get any further with the talking, because something happened. From the spaceship, a black laser beam shot at the warehouse. As soon as the beam touched the building, there was a hissing sound. It was like extinguishing a fire with water. The building glowed and disappeared before the eyes of those present. Only a black pool, which stank terribly, remained lying. After a few moments it disappeared. General Cobe, Sergeant Rock and the soldiers had just seen the warehouse erased by this black ray. "My God," spoke Cobe, "What a terrible weapon".

"Yes, Sir," Sergeant Rock whispered next to him. "If they shoot at us, then—!"

He did not speak any further, because everyone knew what could happen. General Cobe raised his finger to the sky and pointed to the different points that were circling next to the spaceship. Despite the distance, he knew what they were. They were Tiger combat helicopters. These helicopters were planned for the following years. But here they were used earlier. Likewise, some F-15 E fighter planes of McDonnell Douglas flew again and again beside and over the spaceship.

"We'll see what else these aliens can do," General Cobe said.

"But, Sir? They shot at the whole warehouse complex and dissolved it," said Sergeant Rock.

"Exactly! Just a warehouse. Nothing else. Sooner or later someone else would have had to do it. Subsequently, these creatures or whatever did the work for us," Cobe replied. "We shouldn't rush into anything".

"Yes, Sir!" The spaceship was still floating. Now it sank a little. Then, all humans heard a humming noise. The lower part of the spaceship, right in the middle, opened and a weak light filled the hole. The light condensed and a ray came out. It was a milky cone of light pointing to the ground. General Cobe and the others watched with open mouths what was happening.

"There you are, Sir," Sergeant Rock whispered to the General. He pointed to the shadow moving in the cone of light.

"I see it," Cobe said. "It seems someone came down from the spaceship to talk to us."

"I think so too, Sir". The two of them looked eagerly at the shadow, which was more than two meters high. Everyone could see this. But nobody could see the figure vividly. It was and remained stuck in the milky cone of light.

Now she turned the shadow to the person, behind the sandbags and a horrible voice sounded, "We have been able to decipher your primitive language and we ask you only once. Where is our brother?".

General Cobe felt addressed by the Being. He turned to the sergeant and asked for something. He pressed this something into his hand and the general stepped towards the cone of light. In his hand, he held a bar. At the end a white flag waved. When he stood close enough to the light, he spoke to the Being. "I am General Cobe". It was dull in his stomach. To stand alone in front of this Being. The fact that he brought the courage together was a miracle.

"I hold this white flag to meet you. It is a symbol of peace".

"Peace? General Cobe speaks of peace with all the weapons around him?" said the Being.

"It is only a protective measure. I think you would also protect yourself from strangers who would suddenly show up at your place to disturb you".

"I beg to differ. No human has ever appeared before us. They were wiped out before they could". Cobe swallowed the words. "Where is our brother, human?" the Being spoke again.

"I don't know who you are looking for".

"You liar. We have heard his cry, into the infinity of space. This cry came exactly from the point where that man had stood before".

"That was the old warehouse you destroyed".

"Now you tell me where our brother is or this world will be wiped out".

Those were hard words. Everyone had heard them and nobody could do anything. Not even General Cobe. He wondered how he would explain it to this Being but he spoke again, "I do not know your brother, but I know someone who must know something about him".

"Then, bring him to me".

"He is not here. He has disappeared and no one knows where he is going.
The Being in the light spoke no further. He listened to what his brothers said to him from above. After a few moments, he spoke again to the general. "Find him. In the meantime, we will deal with you".

"We...we don't want any war with you. We live here in peace with all people".

"With all the weapons around you? This is over now," the voice came from the inside of the cone of light.

General Cobe slowly stepped back. The flag was hanging down on the right hand. It had become worthless to him. 'What shall I do?' was his thought. 'Only Fenton can give me an answer and he is not here'. He stood by the sergeant again and took his cell phone out of his hand. Then he typed in a number. "Tell all planes to get the hell out of here. Immediately!" he called in. The fighter planes and the Tiger helicopters continued to circle around the spaceship. When the order came, it was too late. From the spaceship, a dark laser beam penetrated. He cut like a sword through the air. In a circle, around the spaceship. Everything that was in the air and could not avoid the laser beam was divided into two halves. The air vibrated as the machines exploded. The screams of the dying penetrated the heads of the soldiers on the ground. Debris from the machines fell to the ground and buried some soldiers beneath them. Fire and smoke rose to the sky.

"They declared war on us," Cobe wrote. The few flying machines in the spaceship orbited their on-board rockets. They also fired with their machine guns. The spacecraft had a protective jacket made of black energy. None of the missiles and bullets were able to penetrate this shield. Everything bounced off. The dangerous projectiles fell to earth and caused an inferno. Tanks, anti-aircraft guns and humans were hit by their own projectiles. Many died under the explosions. Bodies flew burning through the air. Shredded and mutilated corpses paved the streets. Here and there you could hear a quiet whimper that quickly stopped. It was death that blew through the streets. People died by their own weapons. General Cobe and the sergeant had thrown themselves to the ground and protected themselves. They had put their arms and hands over their heads. At some point, they got up. The dirt on their clothes trickled off. Next to the sergeant lay a dead soldier. He had no face. Feeling disgusted, he looked away and stood up beside the general.

A picture of horror offered itself to them. Everything lay in a field of ruins. From afar, they saw fires. The flying machines had crashed into the houses. Whole blocks of flats were on fire. The skeletons of the flying machines burned out slowly. Even from this distance, one could hear the sirens of the fire brigade. All the men heard the crackling of many fires. "My God," the general said. "How terrible." Sergeant Rock was missing the words. He only looked at the milky cone of light. The shadow stood still and it spoke.

"How did you like this demonstration?"

"You" screamed the general, "You are—!". He did not speak any further, for he felt hatred for this Being. Deep hatred.

"Now," spoke the Being. "Have you already found what we are looking for?"

"How shall I do that? You have begun to kill us. We didn't even have time to do anything".

"Then we will continue," said the Being. "We will meet you here on the ground. My brothers want to play with you".

The soldiers next to the sandbags held their machine guns like a lifeline. They knew what was coming to them now.

Chapter 68

Somewhere, on the other side of heaven, evil beings once lived." Erik Fenton had to concentrate so that he could understand his ancestor. "These Beings all had the same body. They were brothers and had the same spirit. With iron ships they flew, like the birds in the sky, to other worlds and extinguished all life. The Nameless one belonged to them. Until the moment when everything changed. One of these flying ships who is smaller than the others, went off course and got caught in the pull of a strange flying stone. The pull was so strong that it disappeared into the tail of the stone. The iron ship came closer to the stone and touched the hot surface. This touch had consequences. The ship and the only evil Being were shrouded in a bright light. It was a few moments, but they were enough to change the evil life of this Being. Evil became good and that was not all. The Being was given unimaginable powers and immense knowledge. This had been caused by the flying stone. As soon as these moments were over, the iron ship could detach itself from the stone, then from the tail of the stone and flew away". Erik Fenton listened to this fantastic story. 'This flying stone could only have been a comet and a spaceship,' he thought. Then he listened further.

"The Being was none other than the Nameless one and had had a goal before touching. He had to explore a planet and transmit it to his brothers. These would then bring death and destruction. Instead, the Nameless One set course for his black planet. When he was close enough, he knew exactly what to do. With the mighty power of his weapons and the bright light he had received, he shot at some important points of his home. No evil creature was to survive. A chain reaction was the result. His home, his home, was destroyed. As fast as he could, he flew far away and saw his world break apart. It exploded. But unnoticed, on the other side of the planet, a ship flew into the sky. The evil Beings followed the Nameless one to kill him. But the Nameless One was endowed with enormous powers and far superior to the others. Like lightning he flew through the black sky and reached the flying stone again. He dived into the tail and was not seen by the persecutors. Subsequently, he drifted through the stars to our earth".

Erik Fenton listened carefully to his ancestor until he decided to ask something, "Was this stone we call Comet, the only time it passed our Earth?"

"No. This comet always passed by here at great intervals. He has crossed the dark sky many times before and has also taken with him the knowledge of the other worlds".

That was a surprise. Fenton understood the secret of the Nameless. 'This is Halley's comet. It appears only every 76 years. No astronomer has found out the composition of the comet's head until today. Only the Nameless one. On his travels, the comet has absorbed all knowledge in space like a living Being and has passed it on to the Nameless,' thought Fenton. He asked, "How did it go on?".

The Viking scratched his beard before continuing, "The Nameless suspected that his evil brothers would pursue him. It was only a matter of time before they found him. Subsequently, he came to earth and hid in a remote area of fjords. That was with the snow-capped mountains that are near here".

"His spaceship is here? Near us?" Erik said in surprise.

"Yes. It's in an ice cave. You can see the mountain," said the Viking and pointed into the dark night. Erik Fenton had already seen the mountain for many days. But he didn't know that there was a spaceship hiding there.

"What happened back then?"

"The Nameless one knew that his spirit was united with his brothers. Therefore, he was not allowed to betray his kin. Otherwise, his brothers would come and destroy everything".

"I believe that they are already on their way here," said Fenton.

"Yes, they are. But the Nameless man took precautions, because he suspected that it would happen one day".

"It's my fault it happened," said Erik Fenton in a low voice.

"Let it be. Don't worry about everything here. You could not prevent it. No use for guilt. It could also have happened to your father or one of your ancestors".

"But it is still my fault. If I had not screamed, then not a part of the spirit of the Nameless, would have been set free". Erik was full of guilt.

The men remained silent until Erik, the Viking, spoke after a few minutes, "As I said, the Nameless one has taken precautions. We are the strength that he needs to defeat his brothers".

"But how is that possible? Why does he need you to face his brothers?"

"He could not do it alone. The supremacy would be too great. Do you still remember the object?"

Fenton asked, "Which I have given you?"

"Yes. This object and its counterpart, which I carry with me, is the key to everything. When the Nameless man landed here with his flying ship, he made preparations. With his knowledge, he constructed a special machine inside the flying ship, as he called it. I didn't know what the word 'machine' meant. But as I said, through this unusual machine, he dared a dangerous experiment. He sacrificed himself—respectively, his solid figure. But before this happened, he had to have someone to whom he could give his remaining strength from his body".

'Oh, it looks like that,' thought Fenton. 'This Nameless one has dissolved or better said, he has destroyed his body. His power or his spirit, has remained and he has given this power to the Vikings'. Fenton proceeded to remark, "That was you. The warriors from the North".

"Yes. We've got his power".

"But how? What happened?"

"It happened the next day, after the pitch-black night. Everyone you see here was on a dragon boat. We came back home from a raid. The fate of the village should be made clear to us".

"What happened?"

"That night, the villagers celebrated a feast. It was a feast of a Viking who had married that day. The food was good and the drinking horns were filled again and again. The intoxicating mead did not miss its effect. In the early hours of the morning everyone lay in their huts and slept through the intoxication. Slowly, the campfires went out. The rest of the logs crackled and cracked in the embers. Two men watched over the village and the sleeping Vikings. The two did not notice that death was flying towards them. The enemy arrows hit them on the back. The enemies had an easy time. During this time, we attacked Danish and British villages. We did not know that they made a pact. They sailed into the fjords for revenge while we were at sea looking at our captured treasures. Death came that night. The men, women and children were torn from their sleep when the huts began to burn. They ran out and were surprised by the arrows. The village burned down and the glow of fire shone out into the black night. A day later, we saw the smoke from the sea. It was a cold morning when we docked. The enemies were gone. The bodies of the dead were left behind. Some had been eaten by wild animals and birds. It was a horrible sight. The village elder had warned me to leave the village. He had had a premonition that something would happen one day. I, Erik, the Viking, ignored his warning and decided to go on raids. I reproached myself. I couldn't undo it. But there's something I could do. I wanted to take revenge on the enemies. The men and I felt sadness, but the hatred for the enemies was stronger and boundless. We wanted to set sail immediately and follow the enemies. But it came quite differently. The strange man had observed everything. In his bright light he stepped out of the forest and walked towards us. We are not scared bunnies. We look death in the eye every time. But here a Being came towards us which we did not know. Some men were moving backwards. Others threw themselves to the ground. They thought it was Thor coming at us or some other deity. Some proclaimed the name of Odin. I was the only one who stopped in front of the Being. If this Being wanted to kill us, it would certainly have done it already. My hand reached for the sword and I pulled it out halfway. The Nameless one spoke to us. But I did not understand his words at first. They were hissing sounds. The Nameless one pressed something against his body out of light and I could suddenly understand him".

'That must have been a speech transducer,' thought Erik Fenton.
"I am the Nameless one,' he said to me. 'I gave myself this name because I wanted to forget my real name and my origin'.

'Are you a god?' I asked him.

'No, I am a traveler. I come from the other side of the stars.'

'Then, you must be a god'. I knelt down before him and put my sword back. 'Get up,' he ordered me, which I did. My men were behind me. They were still reserved, but they were ready to die if the Nameless one attacked me. Godhead or not! The Name less spoke, 'I see that death has come here'.

'Yes,' I spoke to him. 'We wanted to set sail and go after the enemies. You stopped us'.

'You would lose. There are far more than three hundred men'.

'What are you suggesting?'

'Forget those you want to hunt and kill. It would only mean a senseless fight and a quick death for you'.

'Let the murderers of our women and children escape, and pretend nothing happened?!' I shouted this in the face of the Nameless man.

'Yes. You would attain the same fate. But if you join me, you will fight a battle that will bring you fame and glory'.

"Where will this take place?' I asked.

'Not here, not today and not tomorrow either. This fight, if it comes to it, will be fought in the distant future'.

'How far is the future for you?'

'It can be years, centuries, or as I said, it may never happen.'

'But how is that possible? We can't live that long'.

'You can. With my power, you will live until the time when good and evil will meet. So now I ask you the question. Will you follow me? Will you submit to my power and be ready to fight the battle of the struggles?', the Nameless said.

I, Erik, the Viking, turned around and looked at my men. I was the leader of this horde and at that moment I wanted to hear the opinion of my men. 'You are our leader,' said one of my men. He also spoke in the sense of the others.

'We will follow you. Whatever your decision may be'. I turned around and looked at the Nameless man. I didn't know any fear when I told him the answer. I answered back by saying, 'You heard it. My men are ready to follow me and I will follow you'.

'Good,' said the Nameless one. 'Then listen to what I tell you. Learn to understand why I needed you".

Erik, the Viking, was silent for a few minutes until he continued speaking. Erik Fenton listened to him with excitement. "What can I say? The Nameless one asked us to rebuild the ship, the Dragon. We needed space to sleep".

'Oh. Therefore, the closed ship is in Fort Tilden,' Erik thought.

"When we were finished, he took us to his flying ship and showed us what he was up to. He sacrificed his figure in the special machine. At that moment his power, the bright light, flowed over into us. Now we knew what to do. Since we were familiar with the place, we sailed towards the stars in the direction of the snow mountains".

"The area you call Greenland," said Fenton.

"There we found the right place to hide our ship and wait until the time had come".

"It has come," said Fenton. "But I still want to know something".

"Ask me".

"How did it happen that I am your descendant?"

"That's easy. In the devastated village, we found the young woman who had married the evening before. She was lying on the ground with serious injuries. Through the power of the Nameless, she became healthy. I took her as my wife. When we drove to the icebergs, I knew that she was carrying my son. I brought her to a friend so that she would not remain alone. He promised to take care of her and defend her life with the sword. It was the last time I saw her. She knew what to do because a part of the Nameless had passed into her. But we continued the journey. The power of the Nameless made our dragon boat light up briefly. It completely engulfed us. Then a fog developed around us, because nobody should observe our trip. Our story ends here. You know the rest".

It was incredible what Erik Fenton had heard from his ancestor. "But something still remains open".

"What is it? What is this place? These huts and this area...".

"It's an area from the past. We built the huts shortly before our departure, because we knew that maybe we would come here again. The power of the Nameless brought us here. It is a journey in the past. Here we have found our strength again, which will help us to use it in the present. We can also disappear through the power of the Nameless and emerge in another place. I was away once. You remember?"

"Yes. You saved my girlfriend's life!"

Erik, the Viking, nodded. "But now...," he did not speak further. Something had distracted him.

"Do you feel it too?" he asked Erik Fenton.

"Yes. There is a pulsation and restlessness in me".

"The Ungudds are there. They have begun to spread death. Are you ready to face death?"

"Yes, I am ready. But first I want to put on my normal clothes". The two men stood up and walked to the wooden huts.

A short time later, the Vikings stood together. "May the power of Odin, Thor and the Nameless be with us," shouted Erik, the Viking, with a strong voice against heaven.

"Should we die in this battle, we will meet again in Walhall".

The other Vikings raised their weapons. The swords and axes flash in the sunlight. "We are ready for our last fight," everyone shouted. The air smelled different when the Northerners were enveloped in a bright light. The place where they stood was empty. They had disappeared and with them the light.

Chapter 69

The milky cone of light became transparent and everyone could recognize the Being. It stepped out of the cone of light. Disgusted, some soldiers looked away. General Cobe also closed his eyes for a moment. He did not believe in a hallucination. This Being really existed and it was not gone when he opened his eyes again. The Being looked like a big oversized dog. It ran on two bony legs. Equally bony were the arms. The tendons could be seen. The body shone pitch black, as if it had been poured over with a liquid substance. In the right paw the Being held an elongated staff. His left arm was raised over his skull. The paw pulled together. At the sides of the body two more arms with smaller paws grew out. These held something together in the middle of the body. It was a small box on which some lights flashed. This thing was held with a belt running all around the body. The Being opened its pointed snout. Some shreds of skin hung down and fluttered around as it hissed something at the men. The men did not understand what it said. But they saw the huge fangs in their mouths. The eyes shone in a glowing red. This creature was almost skinned from head to toe. There was little flesh and much bone to see. A cold shiver ran down the backs of each of the men. The men were shocked. "It's like a dog. A skinned dog," whispered Sergeant Rock.

"Yes," said Cobe. "A hideous creature for a dog. Pitiful".

"There're more to come," said Sergeant Rock, pointing to the cone of light. One Being after the other came from the spaceship, floating down through the light. In no time, the place was full of these disgusting creatures.

"My God," whispered General Cobe. "How can we defend ourselves?" The Beings looked around and gave each other a sign. All held this elongated staff in their paws. By a movement of the paw, the staff deformed. Pointed spines came out of the sides. The pointed end opened like a flower. In the meantime, the other small paws touched the small box. The paw fingers skillfully pressed a few buttons. The soldiers saw a lightning bolt. These creatures had built a kind of protective shield around them. Nobody could stop them. A hissing came loose from the throat of a Being. It was the signal to attack.

"Take cover!" shouted Sergeant Rock. The soldiers ducked as the creatures fired at them. A black beam came out of the top of the staff. This hit some sandbags that dissolved into nothingness. Behind them were some unprotected soldiers.

"Fire!" screamed General Cobe and took cover. The loud machine guns and ground guns made the air tremble. The bullets and grenades found their target. But without effect. The metallic objects bounced off the creatures. Now a black beam hit two men. They were the two who whispered to each other earlier. They dissolved in a matter of seconds. Not a single cry of pain could be heard.

"Pull back!" cried General Cobe to the men. They started to move backwards without stopping shooting. There were fewer and fewer soldiers. The bullets couldn't harm the creatures. A tank shot a grenade. This exploded in the enemy group. She tore a hole in the floor. Fire, stones and smoke shot up. The creatures that were hit fell to the ground and straightened up again.

"That doesn't exist. That's impossible!" said Sergeant Rock. The tank, like the others before it, was hit by a black beam. It disintegrated. A black pool lay on the ground which slowly disappeared. Now a jet crashed on the floor. It was fired at from the spaceship. Everything in the air was destroyed. The jet burned light-low. The pilot hung sideways out of the cockpit. The fire was so strong that it burned in seconds. Only a skeleton was to be seen.

"That is the end. We will surrender," said General Cobe. "No more shooting!" he shouted to the soldiers. He stretched his arms up to surrender when something unexpected happened. The creatures also did not shoot any more, they were distracted. Something seemed to be wrong. A dangerous hissing filled the air. The Beings turned around. General Cobe and the other soldiers could not believe their eyes. Behind the creatures, a light had formed. Out of this light, shapes emerged that he had seen some time ago. Under these figures, he recognized a man.

He whispered "Fenton".

In the meantime, Erik Fenton and the Vikings were on the journey back to the present. The light of the Nameless led them to New York. To the place where it happened.

Chapter 70

Out of nowhere, over fifty strangely dressed men faced the creatures. Only one of them wore different clothes. The creatures felt an aura familiar to them, emanating from the bearded men. It was a part of their treacherous brother. The soldiers were now unimportant to the Beings. The new enemies were these men. "Brother," hissed one of the creatures filled with hatred. "You hide behind the people. Come out and die". It aimed its staff at the Vikings and a black ray left. He met the Vikings. But without effect. The Vikings stood in a bright light within seconds. The Nameless one protected every single Viking. It was like the creatures a kind of protective umbrella. No one could penetrate it with any firearms. But when both parties collided, both energies were the same. The Beings and the Vikings were, therefore, vulnerable! The Vikings stopped as if nothing had happened.

"Our brother protects these men. This cursed traitor," hissed a Being.

"You, stay close to me," whispered Erik, the Viking, to Fenton. Before Fenton could say anything, the Viking gave the orders to the men. "Olaf, Ingard and Sven. You go into the flying ship. Starkad, Kjarl, Raghnar, Bodvar and Godron, go left. Vigfuss, Fitjoff, Gunnar, Hakon and Snorro to the right. The others, go through the middle". The first three Vikings ran with enormous sentences towards the cone of light and disappeared into it. The three men would clean up the interior of the spaceship. The others would fight the battle of their lives. With thundering voices, the Vikings stormed forward.

"Odin! Thor! Protect us," their battle cries could be heard. The creatures shot at the Vikings. As before without effect. The creatures had to adapt to this enemy. The physical contact was inevitable. The Beings held their staff in the paw. By a rotation the staff deformed. The spiky end closed. The lower side became smooth. A kind of sword with pointed spines out, was now the weapon of the Beings. As soon as the transformation of the staff had taken place, the first Vikings were there. Erik, the Viking, stood in front of a creature and dropped his axe. He split the Being in two halves. These fell to the ground. The black flesh stank terribly. Bubbles formed, which burst open and smelled of decay. Something moved under the intestines. Worms twitched in the black pool of blood. The soldiers, condemned to extras, watched the spectacle and cheered on the Vikings. It was a fight to the death. The disgusting creatures were in the majority. But the Vikings fought for two. Despite the injuries of some Vikings, they fought on. One arm of one creature fell to the ground, the head of another fell. Black blood soaked the ground and mixed with the blood of some Vikings. Some Vikings died with swords or axes in their hands. The place in Walhall was safe for them. The battle dragged on. Erik Fenton fought bravely. Although he had also caught a blow and had some scratches, he did not want to give up. His sword whistled through the air and hit the left paw of a Being. It fell to the ground and was still moving. By turning to the left of Fenton, he stood next to the paw. This one grabbed Fenton by the heel. Without losing sight of his opponent, he struck down and hit the paw. He split it. Then, he trampled on it until it stopped moving. The creature hissed at him to scare him. Fenton knew that he could not show fear and fought on with the sword. Erik, the Viking, suddenly stood beside him.

"We will carry them all to Niflher," he said.

"What do you mean?" said Fenton, parrying a hard blow. The Viking helped him. He wore his iron rings around the pulses. First, he punched a creature in the pointed snout. The creature lost some lazy teeth. Then, the Viking struck. Fenton's opponent was no longer there.

"If I owned the Mjölnir, I would have knocked his whole head off," said Erik, the Viking. The giant turned around. He saw two creatures approaching the soldiers. They were Sergeant Rock and General Cobe. Erik, the Viking, couldn't let that happen. He popped on Fenton. He shouted, "Come on!" and ran. Erik went on his way. He saw what the creatures were up to. They wanted to kill the soldiers respectively; the general and the sergeant. The hearts of both seemed to fall into their trousers. They were afraid.

"Odin, guide us!" the Viking shouted to the creatures. One turned around and tore up the staff. It was of no use. The giant hurled his axe with full force against the creature. The axe split the creature in the chest area. The second creature had another opponent.

Fenton struck with his sword. First, he hit the small paws at the hip, then he parried a sword stroke and continued. From the shoulder to the hip, he divided the Being. "That was close," said Fenton.

The general and sergeant nodded at him without a word. "My heart stood still for a moment," whispered Sergeant Rock.

It was hard for the general to admit this, but he said, "Mine did, too".

Erik Fenton went to his ancestor, who had his axe back and threw himself into the turmoil. In the meantime, the other Vikings fought inside the spaceship. Through narrow corridors, with little light, the three Vikings ran around. The creatures knew strangers were here and faced them. With screams Olaf, Ingard and Sven ran towards the enemy. Their swords whistled through the air and hit the enemy. They also protected themselves from the shields when a staff wanted to hit them. The battle was short as there were only a few creatures on board. "It's done," Olaf said.

Ingard said, "Yes. The flying ship belongs to us".

"Come, let's go back to our comrades-in-arms," Sven made his comment.

The three ran through the corridors and reached the exit. They floated down from the spaceship slowly, stepped out of the cone of light and jumped on the remaining creatures. Sergeant Rock spoke to his superior, "There. You see, it has stopped". He pointed to the jet planes. There was no more shooting at them. General Cobe nodded. He kept looking at the battlefield. The fight continued. The slaughter had however slowly come to an end. Over fifteen Vikings lay lifeless on the ground. Others, on the other hand, kept to themselves the wounds which the abominable creatures had inflicted on them. Only one creature still stood on its bony legs. There were none of the other creatures left. Far away, this creature opened its snout. It threw its hatred at the Vikings, roaring. The Vikings slowly stepped towards the creature and formed a semicircle. They kept their weapons ready for action.

"It's over," said Erik, the Viking. He came out of the semicircle and stopped in front of the Being. The creature was just one head taller than the Viking and was the leader.

"Now you will die," said Erik and lifted his axe.

"You wouldn't dare," the Being hissed at him. His small arms on the sides moved. The paw fingers pressed some buttons on the box. "It is a great moment of triumph for me. You can kill me, but I'll take you all with me," it hissed.

"What do you mean?" asked the Viking.

"My brother, who has been protecting you, should know".

Erik, the Viking, listened within himself and the Nameless one released part of the secret. The Viking took down the axe. The other Northerners also knew and relaxed. Erik Fenton had moved to the side and was in the back of the Being. He held the heavy sword firmly. He did not believe in a surrender of the Being. Tensely, he listened to the dialogue of the two. He also knew why the Viking had taken down the axe. Erik Fenton swallowed hard. His face had turned pale. "Yes, so the tide can turn" the creature hissed towards the North men.

"What is the Viking doing? Why isn't he sending the mutt to hell?" said General Cobe.

"He must have a reason," whispered Sergeant Rock.

"What is it?" said the general.

Sergeant Rock shrugged his shoulders. "I don't know".

At that moment, death came to both of them. The creature was still holding its staff in its paw. He turned it and the tip deformed again. The flower opened.

"You cannot stop me," it hissed, "I will continue having my fun". It turned around and aimed at two men. It was General Cobe and Sergeant

Rock. The black ray came out and flew towards them.

"No!". They both heard a scream. Erik Fenton had expelled him. He was between the Being and the two soldiers. Courageously, he threw himself in between. The beam hit Erik Fenton. He was hit hard and thrown backwards. The power of the Nameless had protected him. The creature did not fire anymore. Erik, the Viking, threw himself forward. Some Vikings followed him. The giant threw himself at the creature and brought it down. The other Vikings were there immediately. They held the creature to the ground while Erik, the Viking, stood up. He stepped towards his descendants. Fenton stood up and wiped the dust off his clothes. "Lucky you," he said.

"Yes. If you hadn't been here then…". The general and the sergeant hesitantly stepped towards him. "Thank you," the general said. "If you hadn't been here, I would have, you know."
Fenton spoke, "Alright".

The general shook his hand. The sergeant also thanked him. Both looked pale. "The general asked, "Was that it? Did we get through it?"

"Not quite," Fenton said. "There is another problem."

"I very much hope that it is a small one".

"I wish it were".

"What is it about?" asked the general.

"It's about the spaceship. It must go away from here. Really far away!"

The general thought about it. Here his military thinking reappeared. "Away? No! We will use the spaceship for our military purposes. Imagine what we could do with it. We could take advantage of the technology and conquer space".

"Exactly! That is what I mean. That's why the spacecraft has to go!"

"That is out of the question. Sergeant, have your men ready. No one may enter the spaceship or approach it. That is an order".

"Sir," meant the sergeant. "Mr. Fenton saved our lives and the Vikings saved the world. The light, or whatever they call it, has protected him and the others".

"It is the Nameless one who has protected us," said Fenton.

"As I said, this Nameless one certainly has his reasons why the spaceship has to leave, Sir. That's why I can't agree to your order," said the sergeant.

The general exercised his power. "This will give you a military aftermath and end in disciplinary proceedings. From now on, you are under military arrest. Guards," he screamed his soul out of his body. "Arrest Sergeant Rock and bring him back to Fort Tilden".

"General," spoke Erik Fenton. "Leave the man alone. He was the only one who noticed that it wasn't you, but us, who were in charge".

"You? You and this wild horde? Don't be ridiculous. This surpasses your imagination. I have laughed several times, but this is the climax of my life".

"Aren't you happy to have another life?" asked Fenton.

The general swallowed. "That's the height. I will...".

"You will become nothing at all, you ungrateful man".

Erik, the Viking, pushed the axe under his throat. "The flying ship will soon fly away". He turned around without taking the axe from his throat. "Who wants to sacrifice himself voluntarily?" he said to his Vikings.

"We will go," said the wounded.

"Well, prepare yourselves for the journey. May the gods be with you. We will meet again in Walhall". Erik, the Viking, took down his axe from the General's head. In the meantime, the Vikings tied up the terrible creature and brought it to the spaceship. The severely wounded disappeared inside. After a few minutes the spaceship floated up. The

Vikings could control it by the power of the Nameless one.

"Stop!" screamed the general. "You can't do that. It belongs to the military and the United States".

"You're mistaken. It doesn't belong to anyone. Only to the Nameless. You, General, would have conjured up death. What you experienced today was only the beginning of the end. It could have been worse".

"Oh, no, just words. What could have happened? You and your men have destroyed all Beings," said General Cobe.

"Unbelievable. This ignorance," said Erik, the Viking. "What about the leader of the Beings? Why do you think I spared his life?"

Before General Cobe could say anything, the giant turned around. He shouted "Vikings," to his men. "We are leaving".

"Sir," called a soldier. He stepped towards the general and held a radio by his hand. He gave it to him. He listened. "What?" he said astonished. "Can you stop it?".

He interrupted the line. "The dragon ship is independent," he announced. "It ran from the stack and moves, as if by magic, towards the open ocean. Not even the hall doors could stop it. The doors were like butter to it".

"That's the way it is," Fenton said. "The Viking's mission is finished". The general wanted to say something when they heard a howl. It was the spacecraft that moved further away from the Earth's surface. Dust and smoke swirled through the air. It stepped out of the atmosphere and disappeared forever into space. Erik Fenton slowly followed his ancestor.

"Mr. Fenton," spoke Cobe. "I expect you to explain why we couldn't have the spaceship".

He turned around and said, "Do you really want to know?".

"Yes," He came closer to the general. Sergeant Rock also stood next to him. Soldiers were on his sides. "Everyone, except the General and

Sergeant Rock, must go," said Fenton.

Cobe nodded to the men. When everyone was gone, Fenton said, "Promise me one thing, General. That you won't do anything to Sergeant Rock".

It was hard for the general to reverse the order. He breathed heavily. "All right, you win. Let's hear it."

"The Beings you saw destroyed many worlds. First, they'll with the others. Just like today. Once their fun is over, they would destroy the planet from a safe distance. No planet has ever survived".

"But you did beat them today," Cobe said.

"Not quite. Before my ancestor knocked him over, the Being secured itself through the spaceship. Should he die, the spaceship would disintegrate into its individual parts. Therefore, it will explode. That means, the earth would cease to exist".

Both of them became pale in their faces again. "But the Being is gone, right? Will it come again?"

"No, it is finally over. The Vikings took him with them. Somewhere outside the universe, they will kill the Being and thus, sacrifice the spaceship and themselves. No living Being in the whole universe should ever be afraid of these creatures again. Now please excuse me. I still have something to do".

"Where are you going?"

"The dragon ship is waiting. I will accompany my ancestor and the Vikings". He turned away and walked towards the waiting Vikings.

"Wait, Fenton," the general shouted to him. "We will be able to locate you on the radar. If you wish, we will have you picked up. OK?"

Fenton didn't listen to him. He reached the Vikings and a bright light enveloped the men. They disappeared. Not two minutes had passed when the general received a message via the radio. He listened, disconnected and spoke to the sergeant. "The Vikings have been seen aboard the Dragon Ship. Fog has formed around the ship and has disappeared. Who knows where their journey will take them?".

"Only the Nameless man of whom they spoke knows that," said Sergeant Rock.

"Yes," said Cobe. "Only he knows that. Come on, there's a lot to do".

Both of them moved and left the scene. The cleaning of the mess would begin shortly.

Chapter 71

The dragon ship glided in the fog through the water. Each Northern Warrior took care of the slightly wounded. "It was a hard fight. We have lost many good men," said Erik, the Viking. "Just like now. Did you feel it too?" he asked. He stood at the stern and steered the ship. Erik Fenton stood with him.

"Yes. The last of the Beings are dead and with him, your men. We have won. Only that counts and nothing else". The two remained silent. They let themselves be driven by the power of the Nameless through the Atlantic Ocean. Sometime after many days, the dragon boat stopped. It was late evening.

"We have arrived. Here is where your journey ends," said the Viking. He stopped the Drakkar at a jetty.

"I feel it too. Our farewell has come. However, before that, I would like to accompany you to the spaceship of the Nameless". The giant said nothing. He instructed his men to stay with the Drakkar. Soon Erik, the Viking, and Erik Fenton walked up the mountain where the spaceship was. After a few hours of steep walking, they arrived. With the axe, the Viking knocked the ice away on a rock face. They saw an entrance into a cave. The two entered after lighting a torch next to the entrance. Fascinated, Fenton stopped. The spacecraft of the Nameless stood in a huge ice cave. Nobody had been in here for centuries. Subsequently, the outer hull of the spaceship seemed as if newly cleaned.

"Incredible," whispered Fenton. Erik, the Viking, stood in front of the spaceship and reached into his pockets. From there he got a leather bag. In this bag was the metallic cylinder which Erik Fenton knew. The giant held it in his open hand. Suddenly, it began to glow weakly. The glow became stronger and more intense. The outer hull of the spaceship picked up the light and a door of light opened. It opened the way into the interior.

"Come," said the Viking and walked ahead. Fenton hesitantly followed him into this strange oval thing. The giant walked through the corridors as if he had been here a hundred times before. Then he stopped in front of a door. The door opened and he entered. It was the control center of the spaceship. "Here, the Nameless one will rise again," spoke the Viking, full of awe.

"What do you mean?" asked Fenton. "I don't understand."

The Viking held the metallic cylinder in his hand. "Centuries ago, the Nameless sacrificed himself. It was his figure that he left. His spirit, his power kept us alive. If I give him back his strength and his body. He will leave us and our world. That's what has been promised!"

"But...but what will happen to you and your men when the power leaves you?" Fenton asked frightened.

"We will die."

Erik Fenton swallowed. "I almost suspected it, but I didn't want it to be true".

The Viking turned around and touched a button on the wall. In the middle of the floor, a cylinder came out. It resembled the one he was holding in his hand. The upper part opened and released an opening. The Viking took the small metallic cylinder and stuck it into the opening. Then the upper part closed again. Suddenly, countless lights on the side walls began to glow. Both men retreated and watched the spectacle. In the middle of the room, where the cylinder was, wafts of mist formed. These began to condense. Even swaths came out of the walls. Erik, the Viking, moaned. It was not good for him. From his body, as well as from all bodies of the Vikings, the bright protection that surrounded them gave way. Only little remained. The light floated to the middle of the room and mixed with the swaths. The room lit up as the light solidified.

After a few moments, a figure emerged from the light. He still has his back turned on the two of them. But now, he slowly turned around and presented himself to the two. It was the Nameless one. Erik, the Viking, bowed reverently before the figure. Erik Fenton remained steadfast and looked at the figure. He looked like the other creatures he had recently killed. Except that he looked friendlier. Not black like the others, but in a bright light. He heard the soft voice of the Nameless one. "It is done. The danger has been banished".

"Yes," said the Viking. "Our task is done. We must go now".

He bowed again and left the control center. Erik Fenton stood there and wanted to say something, but his voice failed. Instead, the Nameless one spoke. "You must be Erik. The last of their line of ancestors. You fought well against my brothers. I thank you! All living Beings in the universe will be grateful to you. I will announce it to them". A tremor went through the spaceship. "It's time to go. But first I want to give you something". Thoughtfully, the Nameless Erik gave something valuable. Fenton bowed reverently to the figure and left the control center. The door closed behind him.

At the exit, Erik, the Viking, stood up waiting. They left the cave and proceeded on their way. The descent was easier. The mountain behind them began to tremble. Stone chunks came loose and rolled down the mountain. The ice above the cave began to glow and burst apart. The spaceship rose from the ice cave and floated up into the dark night sky. Soon, it was no longer visible. The two men arrived at the dragon boat. It stood ready to leave. Erik, the Viking, stood with his men. "Are you ready?!" he shouted to them with a thundering voice.

"Yes! We are," they shouted back.

He turned around and looked at Erik Fenton. "There is no going back. This is our last ride".

Erik Fenton was almost in tears. He didn't want it to be true. "What will happen?"

"We'll go to Walhall. The fog will be our companion on this last trip. The last energy of the Nameless will leave us at dawn. We will dissolve and disintegrate into dust".

"I understand." With sad eyes, Fenton looked at his ancestors. "I will miss you. You and the Northerners. You have all become a part of me. I will never forget you and your deeds".

"I feel the same as Erik," said the Viking. "Not only did I meet my descendant during this time, but I also found a good friend and a great ally. I would swing my weapon again with you at any time and destroy enemies. Unfortunately, this is no longer possible. Now it is time to go. Farewell". The two men hugged each other. As soon as they had separated, Erik, the Viking, stood at the dragon boat and jumped onto the deck. The ship planks trembled. "Forward, men. Row out the fjord. We still have a long way to go".

Erik Fenton stood at the jetty and watched the ride of the Drakkar. He waved to the crew and his waving was reciprocated. Around the boat, fog was forming and completely consummated the boat, never to be seen again. Erik Fenton sat on the jetty and stayed there all night. The morning was dawning. He thought of the men who would soon reach Walhall. His thoughts were interrupted by engine noise. Two Norwegian military helicopters flew in and one gently touched down at the jetty. A little later, Erik Fenton was on board the helicopter.

"How are you, Sir?" he was asked.

The noise in the plane was unbearable. That's why he had the headphones on. Eventually, he could talk to the other man. He nodded. "We have orders to take her to the nearest airport. There she will fly a private jet back to New York".

"Thank you. How did you find me?"

"We had the dragon boat on the radar, so we could follow you," said one of the men. Erik Fenton and looked down. Wherever he looked, he saw only water. His thoughts were still with the Northerners. The helicopter turned left and flew inland. Half a day later, the private jet landed at La Guardia airport. There, Erik embraced his girlfriend Helen Turner, who had been waiting for him. Next to her stood Captain Tom Stone. "Welcome back," he said and shook hands with Fenton. "Now that they are unemployed, I would like to have you back with my troop. Would that be alright for you?"

"I'm thinking about your offer. But first, I will go on holiday for a long time. I have earned it."

The three stepped to the arrival hall and disappeared between the crowd.

Next Time in...

The Nameless II: The Last Brawl

Years later, Erik Fenton caught up with the past.
The inevitable, abhorrent brother of the Nameless has escaped and returned to earth with an army of evil beings, embellished with thoughts of destroying everything that stands in the way. But he had not counted on Erik Fenton and his ancestor. They confronted the power and, with the help of friends, taught the aliens fear.

Will they survive this last fight? Can the assistance of the Nameless be enough to protect them? Let us drift through the power of the Nameless and experience the end of this incredible and terrifying story.

Books by BELLAVISTA

The Warrior from the Past
THE AWAKENING
PAST AND PRESENT

The Nameless
THE AWAKENING
THE LAST FIGHT

Other English Novels
THE BAR

Novels in Other Languages
DER AUSERWÄHLTE (Pub. 2006)